MY DAD'S BILLIONAIRE BEST-FRIEND

AXEL AND CHASTITY

BOOK ONE

LEXIE MIERS

CHASTITY

"**W**ow. Who's the guy? Your boyfriend? He's unbelievably hot!"

I flinched as a new college friend sidled up next to me and sat down on the ledge I'd been occupying.

The man she was looking at was a chick magnet, it was true. With dark, short, styled hair, figure hugging jeans and a washed out vintage band t-shirt a size too small that showed off his ripped muscles.

He lifted his arm and waved at me, a huge smile causing him to flash his pearly whites at me.

I waved back, shaking my head. He wore what he liked, but sure didn't look like my friends' fathers.

"Not my boyfriend, my dad," I said, matter-of-factly as I stood and slung my bag over my shoulder and grabbed my suitcase. "Have a great break."

I walked away from Claire, whose mouth was still hanging open as she continued to stare at my father. I knew all the questions that would be running through her mind. First and foremost, would be, "How old was he when you were born?" I'd been asked the question a thousand times before.

"Hey, Chastity, how was your week?" he asked, leaning casually against his red convertible, like an old re-run of Magnum, PI.

I narrowed my eyes at him. "Seriously, Dad. Can't you wear normal fitting shirts like everyone else's father?"

He laughed and pushed off from the car, his big arms encircling me and squeezing tight. "I've missed you."

I let my eyes close as I inhaled his scent. The spicy Polo he'd been using since I was little engulfed me and made me yearn for Friday night movies and popcorn that had been our tradition. "Me too." I stepped back and he held open the passenger's side door for me. *Always a gentleman*, as my mother would say. Pity she hadn't held on to him long enough for us to be a real family. "Thanks." I slid into the small, older BMW and he got in the other side after closing my door and walking around hood.

"Do I really embarrass you?" Dad asked, his huge biceps flexing as he turned on the ignition and grabbed the gear shift.

I rolled my eyes at him in an exaggerated way. "Some of my oblivious friends think you're my boyfriend when they first see you. They're shocked when I say you're my father."

He chuckled and pulled into St. Pete traffic. "Not my fault I take care of myself and didn't age as well as your mother."

Age as badly, you mean. "Hey, leave her out of it. She doesn't have the time you do to spend hours in the gym, you know," I shot back and then had to work hard not to laugh when he gave me a side-eye look that said, "You know what I mean." I sighed and glanced out the window, watching the palm trees fly by.

My dad wasn't *that* young. I was born on his twenty-first birthday, and he always said I was the best birthday present he ever received. The problem was, I was now twenty-one, and instead of looking forty-two like he should, my dad looked thirty. Maybe thirty-five, if you looked really close at the crow's feet around his eyes. But his body was better than any thirty-year-old I'd ever seen, and his naturally thick and dark hair took a decade off his age.

"Mom isn't that bad," I defended, and my dad didn't say anything, diplomatic guy that he was. "She just looks her age." *Or a few years older*. She worked hard as a high school algebra teacher and was always stressed. *Next topic, please...*

"Anyway, sweetheart... how have you been? I feel like we haven't caught up in forever."

We hadn't. It had been far too long between dinner dates with my dad, which is why I was so happy we were going to spend a whole week together over the Christmas break. "Awesome. I got some incredible news, actually." I turned towards him to talk as he drove.

His gaze flicked over to me, his lips lifted in a smile. "Tell me."

"I got accepted into Sherman."

"For chiropractic?"

"Yes!" I squealed and then swallowed hard to force myself to calm down.

His contented sigh and smile said it all. "Oh, Chastity, I'm so proud of you. That's fantastic news."

Neither of my parents had finished college. When they'd gotten pregnant with me, Dad had dropped out to get a job, but they'd spilt up by the time I was two. Luckily Mom had managed to finish her teaching degree when I got older, but they both missed out on some pretty major opportunities in life, thanks to their promiscuity. And stupidity.

One of the main reasons I did not sleep around. Quite the opposite. "I couldn't have done it without you, Dad."

"Naw... don't be ridiculous. You're a star. And you should shine."

Both of my parents had helped me enormously through school with living expenses, since I'd earned a full financial scholarship for tuition, but my father was always my biggest cheerleader. "Without your help, I could never have studied so hard, Dad. I want you to know how much I appreciate it."

His cheekbones were looking suspiciously pink now and he brushed the back of his free hand against his eyes. "I'm just glad you used that brain of yours for something good. And I hope that means I get free adjustments for the first five years?"

"More like forever!" I beamed at him. I could never repay the help he'd given me, but I'd make sure his spine was in tip top condition for the rest of his life.

He chuckled and turned the car off the street and into the gym parking lot near his apartment.

I glanced up at the large signage. *All Day Health.*

Dad had managed to work his way up through the commercial construction company he worked for and now had an office job preparing quotes and building specs for large projects. He had a nice apartment in an upscale part of town and worked out at an exclusive gym.

"Do you need to lift again before we get home?" I joked as he parked and turned the ignition off.

"Uh, not exactly. I've got a casual meeting of sorts inside. This investor is really difficult to pin down, so he invited me to have a chat after his training. It's a new business venture I'm looking into. Do you mind if we stop here for twenty minutes before we go home?"

I did mind a little bit. I wanted to spend time with him, not sit in the car by myself. "Sure, but can I come inside with you? I don't feel like sitting in the car and frying in the sun."

He laughed that deep, carefree laugh he'd always had. "Of course. There's a café and an area to relax if you want to play on your cell for a bit. I'll show you."

"Perfect." I grabbed my bag and we both got out of the car.

When we walked inside, the air conditioning hit me in the face like a snowstorm. "Whoa, it's freezing in here."

Dad chuckled and indicated I should follow him, so I did.

We walked through a second set of doors and into Nirvana, where the coffee was grinding, soft music played, and I couldn't stop myself from sighing.

"This is awesome." Nothing like the basic gyms Mom and I had frequented over the years.

My father smiled again at me, then stepped over to the counter and spoke to the pretty woman working there. She nodded and he came back to me. "I just spoke to Martine, and she'll take care of you. Order anything you want. I won't be long, Chas, I promise. You all right here?"

In the lap of luxury? Absolutely. "Yeah, sure, Dad. Go. See you in a bit."

He disappeared through the frosted glass doors, and I suppressed the urge to squeal. I'd spent the last few weeks cooped up in a small dorm room studying for finals. This was heaven in comparison.

"Would you like something to drink?" the pretty blonde called out and I walked over to the bar.

"Sure. I know this is a strange request, but a hot chocolate, if you've got it?"

She nodded and went over to the coffee machine.

I turned and leaned against the bar, letting pure happiness filter over me. *When I'm a Doctor of Chiropractic I'll belong to a club like this. One day.*

Growing up with a mother who had very little, we'd never gone on vacations. My father had helped the best he could, and I'd never wanted for anything I actually *needed.* But now, I could see my future ahead and I was sure my mom would love to join a place like this too. I owed her everything. I'd find a way to make it up to her. All the sacrifices she'd made for me. Just four and a half more years of school and I'd be able to buy her all the extras she'd missed out on.

The frosted glass doors that led into the interior of the health club opened and my gaze swung towards them, half expecting my dad to walk back through. My belly tightened and clenched with an intensity I'd never experienced. *Wow.*

The man who walked through the door was sex on legs. Literally. You could feel the intensity of his power like a radiant wave of heat.

Whoa.

His gaze turned my way and sparks sizzled between us. I couldn't move and I couldn't look away as heat simmered through me.

His lips lifted in a smile as he hefted his sports bag onto his shoulder. He seemed to be going for the doors that led to the outside, but then he turned and headed over to the bar near me.

"Hiya, Axel. Ice water?" the blonde woman asked him, her voice strong and overly friendly.

He winked at her and nodded. "You know me well. Thanks, Martine."

I shivered. The timbre of his voice was perfect. Deep and rich. Strong and sexy.

He turned towards me, his perfect white teeth glistening in a smile as his blue eyes sparkled in response. "Here to work out?"

Me? I struggled to think of a response. My gaze was drawn by the thin sheen of sweat on his bulging biceps and I wondered how sweet he would taste. His physique wasn't exaggerated like some puffed-up body builders. But God, did I want to bite those biceps. I shook myself. "Uh, me? No. Just getting a hot chocolate and waiting for my dad." A warm drink may have seemed odd in this heat, but Christmas was approaching, and it was my holiday go-to.

His eyebrows lifted high on his forehead, slight wrinkles at the edge of his eyes indicating he'd be about ten years older than me. Perhaps a little more.

Nothing like a hot, older guy to teach you a few things. Which I needed desperately.

"They sell hot chocolate here?" he asked skeptically.

I laughed. "Yeah. She said they did, anyway."

Martine slid a mug across the counter towards me. "We don't get many orders for it, but I always have some in stock."

"Why wouldn't they have it?" I asked, lifting the mug to my lips, and taking a big sip. "Hmm... Yum."

The man in front of me laughed. "Ah, because this is a health club and most the women here are terrified of sugar."

I shrugged. "Not my problem." I probably carried a bit too much weight by most people's standards, but I did laps at our school pool when I found the time and generally ate well. My life didn't start or begin with my weight. I didn't even own a scale.

He stared at me for a moment, as though assessing my soul. Something I wasn't afraid of, because I was a nice person. Or I certainly tried to be.

I stared straight back at him, feeling a strength building within me. I'd gotten over the initial shock of his devastating appearance, and now I wanted to know if he had some brain cells between his gorgeous ears.

"Yes? Was it... Axel?"

He shrugged. "Alternative parents."

I rolled my eyes. "Yeah... I know the feeling."

He stuck out his hand. "Axel Patterson. Pleased to meet you...?"

"Chastity," I answered and wasn't surprised when he burst out laughing.

"Really?" He grinned, his gaze running up and down my body. "Is there a metal belt hidden under those jeans?"

I'd been asked similar questions in the past, and always tried to have a smartass answer in response. "Of course, I do. After all, we are the names our parents gave us, aren't we? So, tell me, Axel... Do you stick your arms out and act like an axle for the wheels in your car?"

He froze for a moment, his eyes widening in shock before he burst out laughing.

Martine pushed the tall, icy glass at him, her interested gaze swinging between us.

He picked up his drink and downed the whole thing like a thirsty pelican. When he put it down, he was still smiling. "You're the most interesting person I've met today, Chastity."

I snorted. "That doesn't say much for the people you work with, then."

His blue eyes sparkled even more as he stared at me and my gaze swung down to his left hand, bare of a wedding ring. "No. No it doesn't."

2

CHASTITY

Axel flicked his wrist around and checked a very expensive looking watch. "Damn, I've gotta go. But I hope we meet again."

That was very doubtful since I was only here on my father's dime. "You probably won't see me again, Axel. But thank you for the chat."

I gave him my biggest smile and he walked away, shaking his head as though he couldn't believe the things I'd just said to him. The front doors opened and let him back into the sunshine. I dragged myself back to the bar and my drink. He was way out of my league. *As if he'd ever be into someone like me.*

Next to my hot chocolate mug was a large smart phone in a black leather case resting on a black mat. Impossible to see unless you were right next to it. "Shit." I grabbed it up and bolted to the door, stepping out into the sunshine and chasing Axel to his car. His very expensive car.

Fuck. Is that a Lamborghini? Yep. Sooooo far out of my league.

I cleared my throat then forced myself to speak when he didn't turn around. "Um... Axel?"

He turned, keys in hand and a gorgeous smile on his face. "Yes?"

I held the phone out to him. "I think you forgot this."

His eyes widened in surprise, then he took it from me and slipped it into his bag with a sigh. "Thank you very much. I would have been totally lost without that. Damn. I'm not usually so thoughtless."

I waved my hand at him and began to back away. "No worries, you just enjoy your day."

He stepped towards me. "So, you're beautiful *and* honest. Any other attributes I should know about?"

I laughed. "Uh, not beautiful. But thanks, anyway."

"I'd like to see you again."

I'd like that too, but how? "When?"

"Any time. Hang on, let me grab my card." He opened the shiny black car with a button on his keys, leaned inside and came back out holding a small, white card. "Here. Please call me. I want to take you out for dinner and get to know you better."

I took the card and stared at the embossed writing. "CEO of a management company? No offense, Axel, but I don't think you're going to find me very interesting." I had to be honest because seriously, I didn't think we had a single thing in common. Least of all, our exercise habits.

"I think you're wrong. You're a breath of fresh air to me."

I snorted, not sure if that was a compliment. "Yeah, my mom would say something similar. She's always telling me to think before I speak, but my mouth can't seem to slow down long enough for that to happen."

He continued to stare at me as though he'd never seen a person like me before. Perhaps he hadn't.

"Well... I better get back inside." My father may be looking for me as we speak.

He reached out and grabbed my hand, pulling me closer. His fingers were hot and slightly rough against my hand. Strong. "Please say you'll go out with me."

My breath hitched in my throat. He couldn't possibly be serious. But as he waited for my response to his absurd question, my heart began to race inside my chest. I swallowed hard and tried to ignore the way my nipples tingled beneath my plain t-shirt. "But you are so far out of my league," I blurted out, then wished I'd kept my thoughts to myself.

He cocked his head to the side. "You'd prefer me poor?" he asked, kinking one eyebrow up.

I huffed out a laugh and pulled my hand out of his grip. My fingers ached to run alongside his hair and pull him into me for a kiss. It had been so long since I'd felt anyone's lips on mine, and he was attractive in every way possible. "No... it's just—"

He cut me off, not that I had a proper answer to his question. "It's just *nothing*. Go out with me. Your choice. Anywhere you want."

I lifted my gaze and met his solid blue stare. That sounded like a challenge. "Anywhere I want?"

He nodded and butterflies fluttered inside my belly. This could be fun. "All right, I'll go out with you, then. But it's my choice."

He gave me a huge smile that made my knees weak. "You're so delicious, I just want to devour you."

I giggled, unable to help myself as a heated flush raced up my cheeks. "You sound like the big, bad wolf."

His grin was the sexiest thing I'd ever seen, and I staggered sideways, catching myself on a conveniently located pole.

"You all right?" he asked, his smile conveying his humor at the situation.

"Yeah, thanks. I better go." I began to back away, glancing towards the gym, but my father was nowhere to be seen.

"When are we going out for dinner?" he called out, ever persistent.

"I didn't say it was dinner," I responded, laughing inside. As if I was going to take advantage of some rich guy. I'd been taught better than that. Plus... if I even had a chance with a man like him, I wasn't doing what every woman had done before me. I wasn't going to be boring.

His eyebrows drew down in mock outrage. "When?" Axel repeated.

I thought quickly. Dad always worked weekends, even when I was with him. Maybe I could sneak out for a few hours in the afternoon? "Tomorrow too soon?"

"Definitely not. What time?"

I loved how he let me choose everything. For a man who obviously had total control of his life, it was a lovely gift. "Three? I can meet you here if you like."

His lips quirked a little, but he didn't ask anything else. "Done. I will see you, gorgeous girl, tomorrow."

I nodded and took slow, careful steps backwards. I clung to his card like a lifeline. I was not letting it go.

He gave me one more killer smile that made my insides clench and tighten in a way I hadn't felt before. Then he got in his car and drove away.

I wandered back inside in a daze, reaching out for my now barely warm hot chocolate with a stupid smile on my face.

"What happened?" the woman behind the bar asked. She was eyeing me in a way that reminded me of a jealous bitch I'd once known in high school. Her hackles were raised, and her eyebrows were lowered. Not a good sign.

"Oh, nothing. Just gave him back his phone." I wasn't telling her anything. Her mood had changed substantially since my interaction with Axel, and the last thing I wanted was some blow-up from her in front of Dad. I finished my drink and pushed it over the counter towards her. "Thanks so much." I wandered over to the couch and settled down just as I heard my dad's voice over my shoulder. I twisted around to see him deep in conversation with an older man with silver streaks through his hair. They shook hands and the man left.

Dad walked over to me; his smile full of happiness. "Hey, sweetie. I'm sorry that took a little longer than expected. You ready to go? I hope you weren't too bored while I was gone."

I got up from the couch, slipping Axel's business card into my cell phone case. "Nah, of course not. Looking forward to a night of Chinese food and movies, though."

He put a comforting arm around my shoulders and tugged me in the direction of the entrance. "You were? Perfect! Because so was I."

3

AXEL

I tapped my fingers along the steering wheel of my car, a strange excitement bubbling in my gut. I hadn't done anything this impulsive in too long. I'd forgotten how good it felt.

A movement caught my eye and I turned to see Chastity walking into the gym's parking lot, dressed in the simplest of clothes. Blue jeans. A plain, red tank top. Flat shoes. Her long, blonde hair pulled up into a high ponytail. She looked about sixteen, and I hoped to God she was older than that.

A smile tugged at my lips as she glanced around for me. I dated models. And actresses, and basically women who were professional sex objects. They knew the score, and marriage was not on the table. Money, fun, and sex were. And that had been enough for me for a long time. But as I stared at the beautiful, natural girl before me, my heart yearned for more.

She twisted around and spotted my car, her face transforming into a huge smile. She rocked back on her heels and walked over.

I opened the car door and got out, my hands itching to grab her. Pull her close and kiss the living daylights out of her.

"Hey," she said casually as she walked over, a hint of cleavage catching my eye above her red tank top.

"Hey, yourself." I licked my lips and gripped the car door to stop myself from devouring her on the spot. She made my heart pound and my cock ache. That delicious skin surely needed my lips upon it. *And how beautiful would she look spread out beneath me?* I shook my head to clear the erotic thoughts and forced my mind back to the present. "So where are we off to? A late lunch?" I asked, still confused about the time she'd chosen for our first date. Three p.m. was just... odd.

She cocked her head to the side. "Why? Are you hungry?"

In truth, I wasn't. "Not really, but I gave you carte blanche on our activity." And if this were any other woman I knew, we'd be sitting at the most expensive restaurant in the city, drinking French champagne for the rest of the day.

"Good. My dad's in meetings for a few hours, so I have some time. Can we go drive to the beach and have ice cream?"

I didn't know which shocking piece of information I needed to tackle first. "Your dad?" How old was this woman that she still lived with her parents? And did I need to drive her home like... now?

"Yeah, we're spending the weekend together since I don't get to see him much."

Family-oriented was good. I hadn't had a lot of that growing up. "And you want ice cream?" *Of all things?*

"Yes. Is that okay?" she asked, her slow smile making me want to grab her high ponytail and drag her in for a kiss.

"Absolutely. The beach is twenty minutes away. That gives us a bit of time, I suppose." I was supposed to be working myself, but if she had a few hours free to eat ice cream and talk, then I was clearing my schedule. "Jump in."

She walked around the car, nothing in her hands, and jumped in.

"Don't you have a bag?" I asked her. What woman went anywhere without her makeup, phone and purse? And whatever else women hid in those things.

Chastity reached behind her and grabbed a phone and some cash from her back pocket, placing them both on the dashboard. "Got what I need."

I could only nod as I stared at the crumpled twenty-dollar bills and the typical smart phone with a spangly pink case. "I'm not sure I'm going to like the answer to this question, but how old are you, Chastity?" She had to be twenty-one. *God help me if she's not.* I started the car, and she looked my way with a devilish grin.

"How old do I look?'

I groaned. *Oh, fuck.* "About sixteen."

She laughed, loud and hard. "That's good to know."

I waited, but she didn't answer. "No, seriously. How old are you?"

"I'm twenty-one. How old are you?'

Relief flooded me. That wasn't too bad. Legal, at least. "I'm forty." Which was old enough. Too old, if you asked me.

She laughed a bit softer this time. "You don't look forty."

I winked at her. "I work pretty hard at that, so thank you." I ate clean, worked out hard, and was embarrassed to admit that I owned more vitamins and supplements than the local health food store.

"I would have said closer to fifty myself," she said calmly, not a bit of humor written on her face.

I spluttered as I stared at her, my mouth hanging open. "Huh?" Was she serious? How could she possibly think I was fifty?

This time she burst out laughing so hard I saw tears at the edges of her eyes. "You should see your face. Honestly, you've gotta lighten up, Axel."

I pressed my foot to the accelerator and turned the car into traffic, heading for the beach as requested. I hadn't been teased in far too long, and the uncomfortable feeling was like spiders crawling on my skin.

"Axel, you okay?"

I think so. I didn't like to think I was vain... but dammit. Fifty? "Yeah, fine. I just..." I swallowed hard. Humble pie tasted like shit. "I haven't had anyone tell me I look older than I am... ever, I don't think."

She shrugged. "Well, I hate to tell you, but you need some teasing. You take yourself too seriously."

We pulled up at the first set of lights and I turned to study her face. "Well, that's what happens when you run a billion-dollar company."

Her eyebrows shot up in the air and her bare shoulder shuddered. "That must be stressful," she said, not sounding very interested.

Didn't she know what that meant for my life? Or what that could mean for her in the future if we continued to see each other? "It means I can do anything I want, anytime."

She snorted. "Really? Can you go on a three-month trip around Europe? And I don't mean to work. I mean like... travel. Relax. Vacay."

I eyed her carefully, then set off again as the light turned green. I wanted to watch her face during this conversation because I had a very strong feeling that I was going to keep this girl around for a lot longer than a few nights. And I wanted to know how much my money mattered. "If I set things up properly, then yes." *Sort of.*

She snorted again. "No, you can't. And if I ever went overseas, I'd want to backpack through Europe. No swanky hotels, no plans. Just set off and go. Stay as long as I want in any place I liked. No computers, no phones, just adventure. I bet you couldn't leave your billion-dollar company long enough for that."

This conversation had taken a weird turn. "You want to travel rough?" Did women still do that?

"Of course. I want to do everything."

"So, you don't come from money then?" I swear, I felt about five years old when she lifted her chin and stared down at me over her nose.

"My parents worked their asses off to put me through school. Am I looking forward to becoming a chiropractor and paying them back for all their support? Absolutely. But do I think money buys happiness? Absolutely not!"

I continued to glance over at her as we drove. My heart had begun to pound like it was readying itself for a run. I liked this girl. Her conviction, her naivety. Everything about her screamed pure and good, two things I hadn't had much of through my life. The silence stretched until I decided to continue the strange conversation. "It sounds like you had a great childhood, unlike mine."

She relaxed back into the seat, picking up her phone and stuffing the cash into the case. "Oh, it wasn't amazing... but it was okay. My parents split before I even remember, so I was always shuffling between two houses, which was hard. But both of them made it work as well as possible, and I was always loved."

"Hmm, that's better than mine." *What are you doing?*

"How come?" she asked.

I wanted to bite my tongue off. What was I doing, exposing all my history to the poor girl? "Uh, nothing. Tell me more about your parents."

"No, I want to know. Tell me."

I considered the wisdom of my next move. Exposing anything about myself was never a good decision, but being honest was probably the best way to go with a woman like this. I shrugged as I drove, trying to make light of a pretty dark topic. "I barely saw my parents growing up. They had too much money and no time for me. Now they live in London most of the year and I hardly see them."

"So, most of your money is inherited?" Her tone was cold as she asked.

I grunted. "Hardly. My parents believe in making your own fortune. They paid for a good education, then said, 'You're on your own.' And I've been working hard ever since."

She seemed to relax at hearing that. "I like that," she said, then sat up straight and waved her hands. "Not the part about your parents being assholes... that's crap. But I like that you've made your own way. I think that's important."

The atmosphere inside the car relaxed and Chastity stared out the window as we neared the beach. "Could we park near the shops on Gulf Boulevard? There's an ice creamery there that I love."

"Sure." I followed her instructions and pulled the car into a spot near the beach. My breath whooshed out of me as I stared at the crashing waves. The sunlight dancing off the never-ending blue.

She reached over and squeezed my hand. "Haven't been to the beach in a while, huh?"

"Nope. Not in months." Longer actually, but I wasn't admitting to that.

"Great then. Let's go."

She released her hold on me and I gasped from the strength of the tingles on my skin. *Ridiculous.* I shook myself as I got out of the car.

She walked ahead, stepping up in front of one of the small shops and ordered a big waffle cone with three scoops of ice cream.

Damn. The calories...

She'd paid for herself before I'd had a chance to notice.

"What do you want, Axel? My treat."

I wanted to scoff at her, but I could see from her clear eyes, she wasn't joking.

"Uh... what do you recommend?"

"Oh, everything, but this chocolate one is my favorite." She stepped closer and held the cone up to me to lick.

I felt like an idiot but did what she asked. I leaned forward and licked the chocolate ice cream. Dark, rich creaminess exploded across my tongue. I swallowed hard as her pupils dilated. "Yum."

She turned towards the man behind the counter. "Double scoop in a waffle cone, please."

I went to protest but she waved her hands at me, and I was soon holding exactly what she'd ordered for me.

When the guy handed her back her change, I pulled my wallet out.

"No. Here." I thrust some money at the man who'd scooped our cones. "Give her money back, please."

The guy held up his hands in surrender, chuckled and walked away from me.

Chastity grabbed my sleeve and tugged. "Not a chance, I've been coming to this place for ten years and your money's no good here. Let's go for a walk."

The man behind the bar gave me a sympathetic smile and I tucked the cash away.

Fucking hell, that's a first. I stumbled onto the beach, my Italian leather shoes stiff and annoying.

"Let's go closer to the water, the sand's harder there. Easier to walk on."

I followed her like a puppy, unable to resist. *What sort of magic was at work here?* "So, now you've got me here, what are you going to do with me?" I asked her.

She grinned and kept licking her ice cream. "I don't know yet."

A growl rolled through me, and I reached out and grabbed her hand, pulling her closer so that our pelvises met, and I could slide my arm around her waist.

She stared up at me, our gazes connecting like two live wires.

"You are far too much to resist, you know that?"

She swallowed hard. "No one's ever said that to me before."

"Well, they're idiots."

I couldn't resist any longer. I dropped my head just as she lifted her mouth to mine. I pressed my lips to hers and moaned as her heat touched me. The attraction between us roared to life like a log igniting on smoldering kindling.

I tightened my hold on her with the hand that wasn't holding the ice cream and slid my tongue into her mouth, tasting her sweetness. The coldness of the ice cream offset the heat of her mouth and I pulled her even closer, wanting her naked and writhing in pleasure.

I dragged my lips away. "Come home with me."

She blinked a few times then stepped away, her head down.

"What's wrong?" I asked, suddenly regretting showing my hand so early. That wasn't like me either.

She tilted her head to the side. "Let's walk."

She stepped closer to the crashing waves, and I trailed behind her, the cold trickle of melting ice cream flowing across my hand.

"What happened?" I asked. One minute she was as hot as the sand, and the next she was freezing me out.

"I don't think going back to your place is appropriate yet."

"Appropriate?" I parroted. I hadn't heard words used like that in forever.

She turned to me and rolled her eyes heavily. "I met you yesterday.

We've spent an hour in each other's company, total. Is it really your normal practice to take a woman to bed that quickly?"

On occasion... "No, but I thought the attraction between us was exceptional. That you wanted the same thing I did."

"I do... but we shouldn't do that yet."

She was shifting and fidgeting like a kid caught with her hand in the cookie jar and I started to smell a rat. "Look, if this is some sort of play, Chastity, I'm not into games."

"What are you talking about?" She was glaring at me now, but the warning bells were peeling madly.

"If you like playing the role of cock-tease, I have to tell you that's not something I'm into. I like my women willing." Anger was building in my gut like a storm, hot and fast.

"No. It's not that," she said, her voice sounding a little hurt.

"Then what? Because I thought you were different from the other women I've dated. But if different translates into a better liar, then I don't want anything to do with you." Why did they all play the same games? It made no sense. Why couldn't they just be honest?

She sighed and her gaze dropped, as did my gut.

I should have known better than to act upon my lustful thoughts. Served me right to think I'd found someone unique for once.

4

———

CHASTITY

ear poured through me like hot rain, making my heart pound and my stomach tighten. He wasn't going to want to speak to me after he learned the truth. *No way.* "I don't like saying it," I managed to get out, clinging to the cone in my hand.

"You don't like saying what?" he ground out. Everything about Axel had changed and I hated it. His mood. His face.

Why was I suddenly the bad guy here? Obviously, he was used to getting what he wanted, when he wanted it, and screw anybody else. I heaved a sigh and put my ice cream to my lips, licking the rivulets of heaven up with my tongue. A fun date had just taken a terrible turn.

"Maybe we should just go back to the gym, Chastity," Axel said, his voice hard now.

"Okay." I nodded and began walking back to the stupidly expensive car. Why was he so angry with me? I walked past a trash can and threw my still beautiful ice cream in, my stomach rolling over and twisting like tumbleweed. What a waste of money and time. I could have just stayed at home and eaten out of my dad's freezer. He wouldn't have been angry at me.

When I got to the car, I turned around to see Axel still standing by the trash, holding his cone and staring inside the can as though wondering if he was going to throw his out too. "Are we going back or not?" I called out and he suddenly dropped his ice cream into the trash and stormed over to me. "What's wrong now?" I asked, stepping back and away from his unwarranted anger.

"I want to know where I went wrong. Tell me. Please. You seemed so natural and different from all the other women I've met. How could I not know that you were just a tease?"

I put my hands on my hips and glared at him. Obviously, the poor guy had been duped by far too many gold diggers in the past, but I was allowed to say no to sex without being accused of being like them. "I wasn't lying. What are you talking about?" He was just being plain stupid now.

"I mean this," he waved his hand back and forth between us. "The sweet smile, paying for our ice cream. All so you can reject me when I fall for your act. I don't get it."

Now I was getting angry. "Look. Just because I don't want to jump into bed with you after one kiss, does not mean I'm a cock tease, okay? Who the hell do you think you are? Some sort of sex god?"

"No, of course not."

"Then why take such offense because I asked you to back off for a bit?"

"Because I know women. And you had all the hot signals on."

I laughed in his face and squared myself up to glare at him. "You know women, huh? What a crock of shit."

His eyebrows shot up. "I do," he declared.

"How much do you want to bet?"

He pulled back and looked me up and down, no desire or heat in his expression now. "A thousand bucks."

Easy. "Done. Tell me how many lovers I've had."

His eyes narrowed and his mouth flicked into an odd smile. "You won't tell the truth about that even if I do guess correctly."

I leaned forward, connecting our gazes as tightly as I could so he'd see if I lied. "How many men, Axel?"

His posture relaxed and he finally said, "Three."

I kept our gazes locked. "Really? You think I'm some sort of amazing cock tease, but I've only had three lovers? That doesn't add up."

His shoulders slumped a little and his gaze slid sideways. "I didn't say you were experienced; you just seem to know how to play the game."

I put all my anger into my gaze and spoke slowly. "Look into my eyes when I say this Axel, because I know you can tell when someone is lying. You wouldn't be filthy rich if you couldn't. Nod if you agree."

He nodded.

"Look at me."

His gaze slid back to mine, and I was beginning to see the start of regret in his eyes, but I was too angry now.

"I. Have. Never. Had. A. Lover." I took a deep breath. "*Ever.*"

His eyes went wide, and he stepped back, bumping into his side mirror.

But I wasn't done. I put my hands on my hips and glared at him. "And just because I don't want to fuck you right now, doesn't make me a cock tease, it makes you an arrogant asshole." I waited for that to sink in before putting my hand on the car door handle. "Now unlock the car, I want to go home."

"Chastity... I'm so sorry."

"You should be. Because I *am* different and special. I've always known it and so has anyone else who's bothered to spend more than an hour with me. So please open the car door and take me home."

He nodded, pressed a button that unlocked the car, and I got in.

I focused on my phone the whole drive back and didn't look at him once. *What a fucking waste of time that was.*

When we finally pulled into the gym's parking lot, I opened the door with a grunt and got out as fast as I could. Dad's house was only a block away and I needed the walk to let off some steam. Pity I couldn't go into the gym and beat up one of the punching bags.

"Chastity, please stop."

I turned around and crossed my arms over my chest. "What?" If he thought I could be sweet talked out of this, then he was seriously mistaken.

"I'm so sorry I accused you of playing me. I know you weren't."

Oh, so now you're sorry? "Yeah, now you say that because you know I'm a virgin. But guess what? I don't care. You're nothing but a spoiled little rich kid who expects to get everything he wants, when he wants it. Well, let me tell you, I'm not for sale." I turned around and stomped off, anger filling my hands and fists. How could he be so stupid? How could I? I knew better than to trust a guy with so much money and so little heart.

"Chastity, I..." Axel stopped, then held up his hands, palms up, as though he'd given up.

"What?" I demanded.

He pulled out his wallet. "I owe you a thousand dollars. That was our bet, right? I would never have guessed that you were a... were a..."

"Virgin!" I exploded at him. "I'm a virgin, you can say it. You were too, once upon a time."

He pulled out a wad of notes and handed them to me. "Here you go."

I took the money, more because I was confused rather than anything else. "What do you mean? Oh my God. You carry a thousand dollars around with you?" I held it up with both hands. "Wow." This was a month's rent for my mom, and he'd handed it over like it was nothing. Which to him, it probably wasn't.

"I'm sorry, again." Axel said, stepping back.

I groaned, rushed him and pushed the money back into his shirt breast pocket. "I don't want your money."

"Then what do you want?"

The question hung in the air, and I found myself struggling to stay angry at him. "I want... I want to walk home. Thank you for the crappy date. Amazingly, it wasn't my worst, by far."

5

CHASTITY

I turned on my heel and started marching through the parking lot, then down the street. Stupid, idiotic man! He could have called me dumb, or ugly, or... lazy! None of which I was, but still... I would have taken less offense to all those words. But cock tease? He couldn't have been further from the truth. The sound of a car's idling engine hit my hearing and I turned to look behind me.

"Jump in. I'll drive you home."

I shook my head and kept walking. "No thanks. My dad's place is only five minutes from here."

"You didn't answer my question!" Axel shouted out his window.

"Which one was that?"

He stopped the car and got out. "What do you want? If you don't want me for sex or money, what do you want?"

The insult in those words was too enormous to process properly, and yet most of it was directed at himself.

I frowned at him as he stepped closer and swallowed hard. It was difficult for me not to stare when I looked directly at him. He was so gorgeous; he made my brain function in slow motion. "I don't know," I said, not sure what he wanted me to say. When he turned away as though disappointed, I grabbed his shirt-covered arm and turned him back. "But you shouldn't categorize women or yourself in that way. It's degrading, mostly to you."

He narrowed his eyes at me. "What do you mean?"

I rolled my eyes. "Are you serious?" I huffed out a sigh and decided to be embarrassingly honest, which for me was par for the course most of the time. I didn't believe in beating around the bush. "You are insanely hot. And way before I saw your car or your business card, I wanted you to kiss me."

He turned back and slid his hand around my waist, tugging me close. "Then why... I know why." He sighed too. "I'm sorry I tried to rush you."

I cupped his face in my hands. "You are someone I want to get to know, but you need to realize that I've never done any of this before. And I don't want you for your money. Or status. Or whatever. I'm going to make my own money, just like you."

He grinned. "A doctor of Chiropractic, huh?"

I grinned at him. "You a fan?"

He nodded. "Yep. Got my weekly adjustment booked in for Monday mornings, seven a.m."

I threw myself at him, hugging him tightly. I didn't know why, but I had to hold him. I didn't know him very well, but now all I could see were the vulnerabilities he obviously tried hard to hide.

He was sexy, successful and forty. But had he ever been married? Kids?

His parents hadn't loved him, so had he ever let anyone else?

I pulled away and he stared down at me, his eyebrows lowered over his eyes. "Uh... what was that for?"

I swallowed the lump in my throat. "Um... I just wanted to."

"Does this mean I'm forgiven?" he asked.

I bit my lip. "I suppose so." After all, could I really blame a guy who obviously had more scars than a pro football player for assuming I was like every other woman? But I wasn't. And he needed to know that. "But no more second guessing my motives. I'll be honest with you. I promise."

He inhaled sharply. "Okay. So... you don't want to come back to my apartment then?"

I was surprised by the question, but then he followed it with the most gorgeous grin, and I knew he was joking, so of course I had to tease him. How could I resist? "I will... but only for an epic make-out session. Think you can handle the blue balls?"

His mouth dropped open.

I laughed. "Another day, maybe?"

He ran a hand through his disheveled hair and huffed out a laugh. "I can handle the blue balls, but I'm not sure I can keep my hands to myself. I'd want to feel you come around me."

It was my turn for my mouth to drop open.

Axel grinned. "Yeah... exactly."

I pressed my lips together, trying not to laugh. What a thing to say! "Well, how about we try again?" I asked. "Another date? Maybe dinner this time?"

He nodded, straightening up and looking more confident by the second. "Tonight?"

I laughed and shook my head. "Already got plans with my dad. "How about tomorrow night? Or Monday, even."

"Tomorrow," Axel said. "Definitely."

I smiled, then found myself staring at his lips and aching to kiss him once more. "My dad's apartment is just down the block, but..."

"I'll walk you."

"Okay."

We turned and started ambling along the sidewalk.

I took his hand, because... why not?

He stared at me a moment when I did but didn't shake me off. Instead, he gripped my fingers tighter, and my breath caught in my throat.

I was in so much trouble when it came to this guy. He was too beautiful, genuine, raw, and so different from anyone else I'd ever met. But was a mutual attraction enough to keep us together when we were leagues apart in every other way?

We walked the final half block and suddenly we were standing outside my dad's massive apartment complex, and I was thinking of reasons to delay going back inside.

"Well, uh..."

Axel slid his hand up my arms until he finally cupped my face and lifted my chin, so I was staring up into his gorgeous eyes. "I'm going to kiss you goodbye."

I nodded, lifting my arms to encircle his neck and drag him closer. But the kiss was a chaste one, a mere brushing of his lips against mine before he was pulling back. I groaned. "Now, you're teasing me."

He laughed and slowly stepped away. "I'm seducing you. There's a difference."

I pressed my lips together, trying to hold onto his taste forever. "I better go up. Dad will be done with his meetings by now most likely. I'm assuming you don't want to come up to meet him?" I waggled my eyebrows at the billionaire, as the man ran a hand over the back of his neck and stared at his shoes.

"Nah, it's okay."

I laughed aloud at that one. "Too early?"

He nodded and lifted his head to meet my gaze. "Yep. A bit." Then he stared up at the building. "My best friend lives here, actually. It's a small world."

I shrugged. There were hundreds of units in this complex. "Well, next time you're here visiting him, come by."

He nodded, his eyes blazing with promise. "Will do." He began walking backwards, a smile still glued to his luscious lips. "I'd better get going."

I watched him go, loving how young and silly he seemed as he stumbled across the street and walked back to his car. If only his business partners could see him now, all relaxed and embarrassed and unsure. I kinda loved it. "Bye!" I waved at him with my arm over my head.

He chuckled to himself, turned, and walked away.

Damn, he had a fine ass. No man should be that handsome and that rich. It wasn't fair to the rest of the world. With my heart singing, I practically skipped into my dad's apartment building and zipped up to the tenth floor where he lived.

I didn't knock on the door. I could hear him talking inside, through the door, and he had his business voice on. I pulled out the single key in my back pocket and slid it into the hole.

Dad raised his hand in greeting as I stepped over the threshold, then turned back to his phone call.

I went to the bathroom and stared in the mirror, taking note of my shining eyes and my too red lips. "You're in way over your head with this guy," I said to my reflection. And yet I found myself laughing, bubbles of happiness floating to the surface. I shook my head, still staring in the mirror. "This is crazy." I needed a shower or something to distract me and use up all this excess energy. So, I stripped out of my clothes, and climbed into the shower, the hot water beating down on my hair.

"Hey, sweetie!" Dad called into the bathroom, the door only opened a crack. "How was your date?"

I laughed at how excited he seemed. "Been waiting to ask that question for a long time, haven't you?"

He chuckled. "Well, you work too hard. You deserve some fun, too."

I was in total agreement. Squeezing the shampoo into my hands, I worked it into a lather, then started scrubbing my head. "It was okay... but it was just ice cream."

"So? Are you gonna see him again? Or cut and run?"

I weighed how much to tell my dad, thinking about the age difference. Not gonna happen.

"Of course!" Dad said. "I'm surprised you didn't organize something for tonight."

I smiled as I rinsed off the shampoo. "No way. I'm looking forward to our night." I couldn't see his smile, but I could imagine it.

"Thai takeout for dinner?" he asked. "Or you wanna go out?"

"Thai is perfect," I said. "And a movie, maybe?"

"I'll see what I've got. Take your time."

He disappeared, leaving me to think about Axel once more. I'd never met anyone like him. He was extremely intelligent and successful, that was obvious. But he'd worked his ass off to get there, which I liked.

He was also the hottest man I'd ever seen in real life. It was definitely in the body and the gorgeous face, but what I really loved about Axel was his confidence—the way he looked at me. Then, what made me want to curl up in his lap and stay there forever, was his honesty. His vulnerability.

Everyone always said they wanted a bad boy, but that just wasn't right. Girls wanted a bad boy who would change, just for her. That never worked out well.

Axel was definitely a bad boy with the stupid expensive car and black book a mile long. He'd probably had more sexual encounters than I'd had hot dinners. And yet that didn't put me off, somehow. It made me wonder how the hell I was going to compete in his bed and his heart when I had next to zero experience, but I wasn't one to be put off by a challenge.

I conditioned, brushed all the tangles out of my long hair, then got out of the shower to inspect myself in the mirror once more. Being too thin was not a problem for me. My boobs were big, and so was my ass. But if the way Axel looked at me was any indication of what he'd like to see in bed, then he was gonna see plenty of it.

I wrapped my hair up in a towel, my breath hitching in my throat. Damn, I was excited. And I hadn't felt this truly elated in a long time. My focus was so intense at school, I really hadn't stopped to smell the roses much this year. Not ever, really.

Well, Christmas was a week away, and I had a few weeks during winter break to have some fun. Now to work out just how much fun I truly wanted to have with a guy twice my age. I giggled as I wrapped myself in a towel and darted out of the bathroom and to my room. The answer was... plenty. I wanted to have as much as possible, and damn his age, experience, and his money. This was fate, and I was going to ride this rollercoaster out.

6

AXEL

I was an idiot. I had to be. Maybe I should get my doctor to do a psych evaluation next time I had a physical? Because this was a first for me, on so many levels.

I was standing outside a restaurant where Chastity and I decided to meet, waiting for her to arrive. This was not the way I dated. I'd pick my woman up, lavish her with attention and expensive meals, whatever she wanted. They knew the score. That nothing else was on the table except for exactly what I was offering them. A small amount of my time, fun, and sex

With Chastity... I shook my head and chuckled to myself just thinking about her and her name. How apt it was. The girl was a virgin and almost half my age. I should be running for the hills. Scrolling through my list of available lovers and picking one off the menu. I shouldn't be here, waiting, for a young woman to arrive who made me as nervous as a twenty-one-year-old, myself. It was embarrassing and stupid and—

"Hey!" Chastity's voice sounded as she walked towards me, her smile as bright as the sun.

It lit me up and reached all the dark and ignored parts of my soul. I couldn't believe she could make me feel so much. "Hey, yourself," I growled at her, grabbing her hands, and hauling her into my body.

Her arms went up around my neck and she pressed her soft breasts into me, giving me a huge rush of lust, then her lips met mine. Her taste was so sweet. So perfect.

I pressed deeper, grabbing her ass, and pulling her into the cradle of my hips while her tongue swept out to meet mine. I pulled away and stared down at her. "Damn, you burn hotter than any woman I've ever met."

She laughed and dropped her head, then did the strangest thing. She put her arms around my waist and snuggled into my chest.

I put my arms around her back and hugged her. And we stood there like stupid teenagers in love. *Whoa. Back the fuck up there. It's your first official date. Don't go falling in love with a girl who technically could be your daughter.*

"Should we go inside? You hungry?" I asked, beginning to feel even more like a fool for my over-the-top reaction to her.

Chastity pulled back and smiled again. "Starving, actually."

I stepped out of the circle of her arms entirely, tugged on my fitted shirt and grinned at her. "Let's go, then."

She nodded, then her hand slipped into mine and I was right back to where I started. With a clingy teenager who had the ridiculous skill of making me feel like a clingy teenager also.

7

———

AXEL

Not wanting to shake her hand off, I instead rearranged her arm, so she held my elbow instead and escorted her into the restaurant. Holding open the glass door for her, I followed her inside the most expensive restaurant this side of the city.

"This is more highbrow than I expected," Chastity whispered, staring into the dimly lit space.

I looked around and smiled. There were only about fifteen tables in total, which made it quiet and private. Add in the candlelight, soft, classical music, and expensive furnishings, and yeah... I could see why Chastity thought it was special.

"The food is amazing," I said, nodding at the maître d who recognized me who then took us to the table I'd booked. An intimate table for two in the back of the restaurant.

The maître d inclined his head and seated us.

Chastity stared at the place settings and ran her hand over the white tablecloth. "This is way too fancy for what I'm wearing."

She wore a spectacular white cotton dress. It wasn't expensive, that was obvious, but it hugged every curve and highlighted her naturally gorgeous skin and youth.

"You could be wearing a burlap sack and still be the most beautiful woman here."

Her gaze flicked to mine, and a quiver of a smile lit up her perfect mouth. "I wanna say thank you, but I don't know what a burlap sack is."

I couldn't stop the laugh that bubbled out of me. *Oh my God... the age gap. I'm an old man.* "Definitely take it as a compliment."

She grinned at me, pink coloring her cheeks. "Okay."

Our waiter approached the table. "Can I start you off with drinks and appetizers this evening?"

I glanced over at my date. "Let's order now so that we can have a conversation while we wait."

She nodded, and we got into the menu. Chastity ordered a salad, pasta, and asked if dinner included bread and that made me like her even more. She hadn't been lying about liking her food and not caring about the calories.

I'd dated women who said they weren't concerned about their weight, but their clothes, their makeup, their eating habits all belied what came out of their mouths. Actions truly spoke louder than words.

Once the waiter left after taking my order, I sat back and stared at her. "Tell me about yourself."

She shrugged and the creaminess of her skin in the candlelight once again caught my eye. "What do you wanna know?"

I inhaled deeply. "Well... may as well dive in the deep end. I feel totally out of my depth with you anyway, so—"

She laughed and interrupted me. "I doubt that very much."

I held up my hand. "See? Even that. I don't remember the last time anyone interrupted me." Not my family, not my friends, certainly not my work colleagues.

She giggled and reached for her glass of water as the waiter delivered our salads. "Sorry. What did you want to dive into?"

I raised an eyebrow at her as I hesitated a few seconds until he left the table. "I want to dive into you... but that's not on the table at the moment."

She burst out laughing, chuckling so loudly everyone around us started to stare.

But I didn't worry about their looks. Instead, I found myself puffing up my chest in pride, since I was the one sitting there with such a beautiful young woman.

When she finally stopped laughing, she ended up taking another gulp of water and wiping the tears from her eyes. "You're relentless, aren't you?" She tucked into her salad, obviously enjoying it, if the expression on her face was anything to judge by.

I nodded, sobering. She had no idea. "Yes, I am. You should know that. It's part of what makes me successful." The greens I started to chew didn't affect me the same way. Chastity was my sole focus.

She nodded, smiling brightly. "I must admit I've been told I'm the same. No one thought I'd get into college, and now chiropractic school. Being stubborn and relentless regarding things that are important, is... well, important."

I nodded at her. I'd never heard anyone so young speak so maturely. "Absolutely."

Our main courses were served a few minutes later and the waiter poured us a glass of red wine each.

Chastity took a sip, then picked up her fork, digging into her gnocchi with a satisfied groan. "God, this is delicious!"

"Told you the food was amazing."

She sprinkled parmesan cheese over her dish then raised her eyes to mine again, "You still haven't told me what you wanted to dive into."

I picked up my knife and fork to start on my filet, deciding to once again jump in the deep end and start the conversation with the only topic I had any interest in. "I want to know why you're still a virgin."

CHASTITY

I reached over and picked up my glass of red wine, taking a slow sip before setting it back down again. I was thrilled that I did it without spilling a drop, though I barely tasted the alcohol as I swallowed it down.

Could he have possibly chosen a more embarrassing topic? *Because he's a horny man! Why else?* "Uh, why?"

He cut into his steak and chewed, appearing thoughtful. "What do you mean why? It's a pretty important question, I think."

I shrugged. "It's not that interesting."

His eyes gleamed as he ate, and I wondered what he was thinking but was afraid to ask. He'd probably tell me sooner rather than later. The guy didn't exactly have any shame.

May as well tell him the truth. "Well... I suppose I never met anyone I wanted to go to bed with."

Axel gave me a look that reminded me of a principal who wasn't impressed with his student. "I find that very difficult to believe."

I reached for the wine again, this time taking a longer sip and enjoying the foreign taste and slight burn. "Well, look. I've never really over-analyzed it, but it probably has something to do with my parents."

"How so? Are they extremely religious or something?"

I laughed at that. "Hardly! No, it was just... they got pregnant with me when they were young, and it wrecked a lot of things for them. Dad didn't get to finish college, and neither of them ever married again or had any other kids. I just feel like... you shouldn't have sex with someone unless you're willing to pay the ultimate price of that mistake."

When I saw Axel's gaze become shuttered and his head bent to focus on his food, I knew I'd said too much.

I rushed to reassure him. "I didn't mean it like that."

"Like what?" he asked.

"Like... that I won't have sex with you unless you're willing to have a baby with me. That just sounds crazy."

Axel picked up his own wine glass, his eyes shimmering with an intensity I couldn't quite make out. "What do you mean then?"

I sighed. "Look. I take sex seriously because it's something serious. The consequences can be extreme in some cases. And I'm not an irresponsible person. I'm sorry if you find that a turn-off." I set my glass down and pushed my unfinished meal forward. Why did every conversation with this guy turn into something uncomfortable?

"I think we need to get out of here," Axel said suddenly.

I glanced up. "Are you serious?"

He nodded, "Just for a minute. Would you come outside with me?"

I nodded, my face heating with shame. What the hell was wrong with me? Why did I have to be so fucking honest all the time? I could have just said that all the guys at school were creeps, and I was waiting for someone who at least turned me on enough to part with my virginity.

I stood up and heard Axel say to one of the staff, "We're just stepping out for a moment, we'll be back in a few minutes."

Then he set his hand on the small of my lower back and escorted me out of the restaurant and around the corner.

8

———

CHASTITY

"I'm sorry... really..." I began to explain, but as soon as we'd stepped into the alley next to the restaurant and no one could see us anymore, Axel was pushing me up against the brick wall, his delicious body pressing into mine.

"Do you know how fucking hot you are?" Axel ground out, his lips speaking directly into my ear.

He slid his hand up my ribcage, grazing my breasts, then moving up my neck until he gripped my jaw and held my head in his hands.

I swallowed hard, feeling trapped. Possessed. And in need. "I thought you didn't like what I said," I whispered back.

He groaned aloud this time and thrust his body against mine. "A part of me didn't. That educated, damaged, hardened part of me that's been screwed over by women time and time again is telling me that this is just a game you're playing. That you're really saying that if I take your virginity, then I owe you. Marriage, children, money—whatever it is that you really want."

Tears sprang to my eyes, and I swallowed hard before I could speak again. "That's not true. You're the one chasing me, not the other way around."

"I know," Axel said into my ear. "And if you can't feel how much I want you, then something's wrong."

He thrust his hips against me again, and heat unfurled inside my belly. Oh, I could feel it. The hard-on was obvious.

"Then how come—"

"Because that's only one voice in my head. The other part of me, and the part that I'm more inclined to listen to at the moment, loves the fact that you are so fucking honest. And sincere. And responsible, and unlike any other woman I've ever known."

I nodded, not sure what to say but hoping he'd keep talking.

Axel pressed closer, sliding his thigh between mine and pressing on my clit with perfect precision.

I gasped and grabbed for him, wanting to thrust back against him but afraid of setting fire to my panties in the process. "Then why..."

"Why, what?" he repeated. "Why don't I just take you home and fuck you right now? I'd love to, as you can tell."

"No. Why did you seem so angry inside?" I whispered, turning my face closer to his, needing to be kissed.

He pulled back slightly so that I could see his eyes and he stared at me. "I'm not angry with you, I'm intrigued by you. I'm confused by you, but I'm not angry."

"But why—"

He kissed me so hard and fiercely; I lost my breath.

Then I was kissing him back with all the pent-up passion in my soul. I thrust my tongue into his mouth and opened my mouth for him to kiss me deeper.

He held my face and I grabbed at his waist, wanting him naked, wanting to touch his skin. Then he stepped away from me, and he was breathing like he'd just run a marathon. His hair was disheveled as he ran his hand through it, and my mouth felt swollen and bruised. He stumbled back another step. "Damn woman, what are you doing to me?"

I took his question to be rhetorical because I didn't have an answer for him.

"I just want to ravage you... you have no idea."

I did have some idea. My panties were soaked, and my heart was thumping in my chest. I wanted him so much it shocked me. "I'll go home with you tonight, if you still want me to."

Axel stared at me, his eyes blazing with heat. Then he stepped back into the darkness with me and kissed me again.

9

AXEL

I kissed her gently this time. Sipped from her lips as though drinking a fine wine. I had to calm the fuck down. She'd just offered to come home with me, and I knew what that meant. She was offering me her virginity, which I couldn't just take.

She'd waited this long for a reason. She'd hadn't thrown it at her high school sweetheart, nor fallen into bed with some drunken frat boy at school. She'd wanted her first time to be special, and I needed to work out how serious I was about this girl before I took something from her, I couldn't give back.

I drew back and stared down into her dazed eyes, then slowly pulled right back. "Should we go back in and finish our dinner?"

She nodded and I reached out and took her hand. She intertwined our fingers, and we walked back into the restaurant, finished our main courses, then moved onto dessert.

We avoided any heavy topics, talking only about college and travel. She had done practically none, so I told her about Paris, Italy, and Spain. We chatted and laughed, ate our decadent desserts, and I couldn't remember feeling so happy in a long time.

When I'd paid we walked out into the cool night air. "So, what are your plans this week?" I asked as we moved towards my car.

"Nothing much," she said. "I'm on Christmas break for a couple of weeks, so I'll just alternate between Mom and Dad's places, see some friends, then it's back to school for my final semester."

So, I only had a few weeks with her before she disappeared forever. "Do you want to go out tomorrow? Maybe we could try the beach and ice cream date again?"

She grinned. "I'd love that, but what about tonight?"

Her eyes were so big and hopeful, I knew I had to be extremely cautious about how I said this. The last thing I wanted was for her to feel rejected.

"I think tonight I should take you home..."

Her face fell like I'd kicked her puppy.

I gently grabbed her chin and tilted her face so she could look into my eyes as I spoke. "Listen to me, beautiful girl. I want to get to know you, and I want you to get to know me. If I take you to my bed, I never want you to regret it."

"I wouldn't," she assured me, shaking her head.

"You would if the next day we decided to end it, wouldn't you?"

She bit her trembling lip, then nodded suddenly. "Yes."

"So before either of us commits to this any further, let's hang out a bit more, okay?"

"Okay," she whispered.

"Hey," I said to her, needing her to understand. "I'm not saying no. I'm just saying not yet. We have two weeks before you head back to college, yeah?"

She nodded.

I grinned at her. "Do you think I'm worth waiting two weeks for?"

The question should have been ridiculous but instead, she pouted. "Don't wait the whole two weeks, because then we won't have more than one or two times. I'd rather we start sooner so I can get good at it."

I groaned and pressed her into the wall. "Fucking hell, beautiful.

You'd test the patience of a saint. Maybe taking you back to my place wouldn't be such a bad idea."

When her face lit up, I knew I'd said the right thing. *Fuck.* "But we are not having sex, got it?"

"Everything else, though?" she asked, throwing her arms around my neck, and clinging tightly to me.

Oh my God. I don't have the strength for that.

I nodded. I'd keep my pants on. That would be the only way to make sure that I didn't take her. Though, even that was going to be pure torture. Penance for the sins of my past. Would she like my fingers? Or my mouth on her pussy more? Or would she only come on my cock?

Heat flushed over my whole body, making my face burn and my cock throb, and by the time I'd gotten her into my car, I was going out of my mind wondering how she'd look stretched out on the bed beneath me.

I grabbed her hand and tugged her away from the alley. "Time to go."

"How far is your place?" Chastity asked as we took off in my car.

I reached over for her thigh, gripping her warm skin, and squeezing gently. "Not far. Ten minutes, maybe."

She shivered and clung to my hand as we drove.

We didn't speak, and it only built the tension higher. Tighter.

How was this the same girl who'd rejected my advances yesterday? Had so much changed between us that she was now willing to jump into bed with me?

I glanced across at her, afraid to speak in case I broke the unbearable tension aching between us, but I had to know.

"Why now?" I put on my signal and turned on to my street.

"What do you mean?" she asked, glancing across at me.

"Yesterday you were horrified by my suggestion we should go to my place. What changed your mind?"

She glanced out the window, then back at me. "Well... I think it's the fact that I've never wanted anyone the way I want you. And I always promised myself that if I felt this way, I'd go for it, and I wouldn't let fear hold me back."

A strange lump formed in my throat. The trust she was offering me was insane. "Thank you."

She grinned at me. "Don't thank me yet, I haven't done anything worthy of it. Not so far, anyway."

My cock throbbed at the mere mention of what was to come.

10

———

AXEL

I drove into the parking lot and pulled into my spot. "We're here."

She nodded. "Okay." She opened her door and got out of the car before I was able to get around the hood to her. She shivered in the cool air of the parking lot. "I know this is all swanky and nice, but don't you ever want to live in a house?"

I locked the car, wrapped my arm around her and hustled her over to the elevators. "A house? As in..."

She laughed. "As in a house. With land around it. A fence. A backyard."

"In the suburbs?" I asked. "Not really."

When the elevator doors opened, I hustled her inside and we rode up to the top floor of the building.

"The penthouse? Really?" she asked, gaping when she stepped out of the elevator and straight into my apartment. "This is unbelievable." She walked around the open plan living area with the huge leather couches and high-end, modern kitchen.

"It's just an apartment."

"Really?" she asked, her eyes wide and disbelieving.

46

"If you don't like it, we can go to another one. There's a few vacant."

"And you own all of them, I guess?" she asked, her tone teasing.

I didn't respond because the problem was, I did own them all. I'd built them.

Her gaze snapped to mine, then her mouth dropped open. "You're kidding me?"

I shrugged. "Told you I was rich."

She groaned and covered her eyes with both hands so she couldn't see me anymore. "What am I doing? You are so out of my league."

I laughed at her and tugged at my tie. It was time to get naked. "Not tonight, I'm not."

Dropping the tie to the floor, I slowly unbuttoned my shirt, not breaking eye contact with her the entire time.

She licked her lips as I tugged my shirt off and tossed it over the nearest couch.

The way she looked at me with eyes as big as saucers and yet with a hunger that was so honest and pure was like a gut punch of the best kind. My breathing became ragged. I kicked off my shoes, then stopped undressing. My control in bed was superb, but I could already tell this girl was going to be the death of me.

She watched me walk towards her, her gaze scanning me like she'd never seen a half-naked man before. And she probably hadn't.

"Like what you see?" I asked, reaching for her, and pulling her into my arms.

Chastity's hands went straight to my chest, laying her hot little palms against my pecs. She grinned at me. "You know you're gorgeous. You must get told that all the time."

I did, and it meant nothing to me. I grabbed her ass and pulled her into the cradle of my hips, wanting her as close as possible. "I want you to want me, Chastity. I don't give a flying fuck about what anyone else thinks. What do you think?"

She giggled and pressed her lips to the base of my throat. A groan escaped me as she whispered, "I think you're the most beautiful man I've ever seen."

Well, what was a man to do when a woman said something like that? I swept her up into my arms, ignoring the squeal that echoed through the living room, and walked her down the hall to my bedroom.

"Where are we going?" she asked, grabbing tightly to my neck.

"My room." Enough talking for the moment. I took her lips in a kiss to keep the fire burning between us. It had been a very long time since I was with a woman as inexperienced as Chastity. Probably twenty years. I set her on her feet, so she was soon standing in front of me again. "Your turn."

"My turn?" she repeated, her eyebrows raised in silent question.

I nodded and slid back until I hit the end of my king size bed and sat down on the luxury mattress. "Yes. Your turn to strip. Show me that gorgeous body of yours."

She covered her face with her hands as though embarrassed.

I waited because I was convinced that she would do it if I waited long enough.

Eventually her hands came down and she took a deep, steadying breath. "Okay." She started to unbutton her cotton dress, one slow button at a time.

I wanted to reach forward and yank the thing off her, but instead I leaned back on my hands and watched the butterfly emerge.

Chastity looked down at her feet as she slipped the dress off her shoulders, then flicked off her white sandals and stood in the middle of my bedroom in only her underwear.

There's a joke that goes, "If you get a woman naked and she's wearing sexy, matching underwear, then sex was her idea, not yours." Well, beneath her gorgeous cotton dress, Chastity wore the most perfectly virginal set of matching lace panties and bra.

And the fact that she may have planned for the night to go exactly as it was about to go wasn't a turn-off. In fact, it made me want her even more.

CHASTITY

I was quivering, quite literally, standing in the biggest bedroom I'd ever seen, in my underwear. I'd worn the nicest bra and panties I owned, and they felt as odd and uncomfortable as a thong up my butt. I wanted to take them off. Now. I took a step towards Axel where he sat on the bed, his hot gaze on my body. He was the sexiest man I'd ever seen, leaning back on his arms, displaying his chiseled chest and arms for me to see.

He seemed completely unaffected by what we were doing, whereas inside my belly, I was a quaking mess. Taking another step closer, I moved between his spread legs.

He sat up, putting his hands on the sides of my thighs, running his warm palms up to my ass.

Setting my hands on his shoulders and staring down into his dark eyes, I forced myself to breathe. To not freak out. I was finally here. With a man I lusted after so much I wanted to go to bed with him. For a moment I wondered how he felt about me then quickly dismissed that thought. The only thing I ever wanted for myself was to not regret my first time, nor the person it was with. And with Axel, I knew it would be perfect.

He grabbed my ass tighter with his hands and I leaned down to kiss him, moaning as he lifted his head and met me halfway.

I kissed him, loving the way his strong lips met mine, then he took over the kiss, pressing my lips apart and tasting me with his tongue. The need to get closer took over. I pulled back and lifted my legs to either side of him so that I could straddle him and wrapped my arms and legs around him.

He grinned like he'd won the lottery and wrapped his arms around my body, taking my mouth in another kiss.

This went on and on, his hands roaming all over my body. He cupped my ass, then moved around to my breasts, tweaking my nipples, and teasing my skin with long touches until I was wiggling and thrusting against him, anxious for a deeper touch.

He spun us around and I ended up on my back, him between my thighs, bearing me down.

This was exactly what I needed.

He moved down and away, then stood up.

I got up on my elbows, wanting him back down on top of me. "I hope you're not planning on stopping there?"

He shook his head, the cheekiest grin on his lips. "Hardly. I just want you comfortable, so how 'bout you shuffle up and put your head on the pillow?"

I nodded and did exactly what he suggested, scooting up the middle of the huge bed until my head rested on a pillow and all I could hear in the room was the thud of my heartbeat in my ears.

He prowled across the bed towards me, but instead of laying back down over me like I was hoping, he reached out and grabbed my panties by the waistband.

"These are sweet, but I'd rather see what's underneath," he said, a deep growl beneath the words making me shiver.

My comfort level was faltering. In fact, I opened my mouth to ask him to turn the lights off, but I silenced that insecurity with an internal whack, swallowing down the protest. Instead, I lifted my hips and let him pull my panties down over my hips and thighs, then lifted my feet as he pulled them off completely and tossed them over his should in a totally slick move. "Done that a few times before, have you?" I asked, then instantly wanted to slap myself in the forehead. "I'm sorry... no, don't answer that."

He grinned and didn't say anything, which niggled in the back of my head. But then again, would I really want some forty-year-old virgin introducing me to the pleasures of the flesh? Probably not. I forced myself to concentrate not on Axel's past but instead, our mutual future.

He slid down onto his muscled abdomen and crawled up over me, kissing my lips then my neck, groaning in my ear. "God... you feel so good."

Then he was gone again, trailing kisses down my chest, over my belly and between my legs. *Oh, shit!* I reached down to grab hold of his hair, to drag him back up and away from there.

But he didn't move as I tugged at him. Instead, he pushed my thighs apart and licked me.

Pleasure shot through me unlike anything I'd ever felt. Then he did it again, and I fell back on a moan. "Oh my God." I felt more than heard him chuckle as he pushed my thighs apart, and this time I let him.

He kissed the inside of my thighs, the fluttering of his tongue over my clit very much like a butterfly.

I gasped and moaned, then covered my mouth with both of my hands to smother all the embarrassing noises. But Axel didn't stop. Instead, he added his hands into the pleasuring mix and slid a long finger up inside me, making me scream out.

But I didn't want him to stop. No... I *needed* him to keep going. Keep feeding this flame of passion inside of me.

Axel drove his finger up inside me over and over again, mimicking the action I assumed his cock would one day make.

"Ahhh!" I called out as my stomach tightened and my legs began to tingle. I was going to orgasm, and I'd never done it with another person in the room before. I didn't know how to let go, how to do this.

Then Axel looked up and grinned at me. "You going to come for me soon?"

I nodded and he dropped his head, suckling on my clit and stroking those places inside of me no one had ever touched before. I crested up to that pleasure palace, then fell again. Everything tightened inside of me and released. I groaned in frustration, unable to hit that elusive level of ecstasy.

But Axel didn't stop. Instead, he seemed to add another finger, stretching me and thrusting in and out of me. His tongue was magic, working over my clit until finally... finally... my legs tightened.

I grabbed for his head and held on tight as my pleasure crested and crashed, and everything went silent and still and tight. And then I was shaking, and coming all over his hand and face, unable to stop the moans or sobs coming from my own mouth.

When it was over and I was left as nothing more than a shivering pile of jelly on his bed, Axel slid up the mattress and pulled me into his arms, my head on his chest, and his arms around me.

I closed my eyes and listened to his heart beating, feeling his warmth around me, and I went to sleep.

11

AXEL

I ran my hand down Chastity's body, enjoying the softness and the sheer lushness of her curves. God, she was so damn hot. And not in a way I normally experienced. She was so honest about her passion. Guileless. She wasn't trying to be sexy; she just was. She wasn't trying to impress me, she was just...Chastity. And she was perfect.

I glanced down at her face where she rested on my chest, surprised she wasn't complaining about the beating of my heart. It must sound like a jackhammer beneath her ear. Pushing back her hair from her face, I glanced down at her again to see her eyes closed and her mouth slightly open, and I had to stop myself from laughing aloud. She was asleep!

The urge to laugh was strong, but I didn't want to wake her. Instead, I'd lie here with throbbing blue balls. A laugh stuck in my stomach, making me gasp for breath. Fuck, she was funny. I lifted my hand and stroked her hair again, closing my own eyes for a moment. I never slept next to the women I had sex with. I had a separate bedroom exactly for this situation.

Sleeping next to those hook-ups was an uncomfortable complication I didn't need. Not to mention I couldn't get a decent night's sleep. I'd tried several times before, and it always ended the same way. With me getting up at four a.m. because I'd barely slept a wink.

My routine was consistent. I'd get up, take a shower, say good night, and settle into my guest bedroom. I wasn't rude enough to ask them to leave. They were always blissed out and comfortable, so I just left them there.

But this was nice. I didn't feel that urgent need to climb out of the bed and run to the shower. I felt content, considering nothing had happened for me except pleasuring Chastity. And, God, had that been amazingly hot. Incredible, actually.

Smiling, I relaxed into the pillow, letting myself enjoy the feeling of her sleeping on me for a minute. I promised myself I'd get up and move soon, but for the moment I wasn't going anywhere.

WHEN I WOKE up in the morning, I was confused. I was lying on my side, the blankets covering me, and in my arms was Chastity. My arm was wrapped around her waist, and her naked body was pressed against me. I froze. How on earth had that happened? Surely, it couldn't be morning. I must have just dozed off for a few hours, and the light in the room was coming from the bathroom or something.

I lifted my head and looked across Chastity's naked shoulder and peered at my alarm clock—six forty-nine a.m. *No way.* I let my head fall back onto the pillow, an avalanche of emotions pummeling my system. What did this mean? Surely, it was just a mistake. A coincidence. This couldn't be the woman I was meant to be with. It was impossible. She had her whole life ahead of her. School. Travel. Work. Kids.

I'd done it all already, except for the marriage and kids part. I'd skipped that intentionally, and I wasn't sure it was a life goal I had anymore. I lifted my arms from her warm flesh and slowly rolled away.

Part of me had always thought that the woman I could sleep next to all night would be the woman destined to be my wife. After all, for me, being able to sleep next to a woman meant I trusted her. It meant that I was safe to relax around her. And that had—literally— never happened with another woman.

I grabbed my cell phone and moved to the bathroom, scrolling through my hundreds of emails, texts and messages. It was Monday and I had to work today. In fact, I was already late for my training session at the gym.

I went to the toilet and jumped in the shower, scrubbing myself clean. What was I going to say to her this morning? I had no idea. I couldn't give her my normal "Thanks, see you around" speech. For one thing, I hadn't had enough of her yet. Yes... yes... that was it.

This uncomfortable feeling was only because I hadn't fucked her yet. Once I did—well, maybe more than once—I'd feel better. As though I could let her go and not look back. The feeling of being out of my depth was unusual. It didn't happen in business, and certainly not in my personal life.

The bathroom door opened, and Chastity suddenly walked in. The cotton dress she'd worn last night had been donned again, and I felt an instant kick of disappointment that she'd covered herself up.

I poured some shampoo into my hand and started scrubbing my hair. "Take your dress off and jump in. I'm sure you could use a shower after last night."

She wrapped her arms around her torso self-consciously and stared at the tiles on the floor. "I am so sorry about last night. About falling asleep. I can't believe I did that."

I laughed. "It was a compliment, don't worry. I was glad that I could pleasure you like that."

Her head came up and she stared at me as though assessing my honesty. Then a small smile curled up her lips. "Well, I owe you an orgasm."

I burst out laughing. Damn, she was refreshing. So honest. So open.

"Deal," I said, gesturing to her again. "You sure you don't want to join me?"

She shook her head. "No. I've gotta get home, actually. My mom and I have plans today, so I better run."

That was usually my line—not the part about parental commitments—but I was definitely the one who would normally be running in the opposite direction after a one-night stand.

"Well, when am I going to see you again?" I persisted, walking over to the open doorway in my shower.

Chastity's eyes ran greedily over my naked body, lingering on my cock so long that I started to thicken and harden in response. She took a step backwards and her gaze flicked up to mine. "Um... when do you want to see me again?"

"Tonight?" I asked, mentally screaming at myself to stop plowing forward so hard at this woman. I was acting like a bull in a China shop.

Then she smiled, and I forgot why I was trying to play it cool. "Okay. I'd love to."

"So, I'll pick you up?" I asked, trying to remember what I had planned tonight. Nothing I couldn't reschedule, I hoped.

She nodded. "Okay. But I'll be at my mom's place, which is about twenty minutes from here."

"I think I can manage that," I said. "Dinner?"

She chewed on her lips. "Uh... I think Mom wants to have dinner and celebrate my getting into Sherman. How about drinks after?"

I crossed my arms over my chest, loving the way her gaze kept wandering over my body. "Sure. I'll pick you up around nine, nine-thirty. Can you text me the address?" That would give me enough time to finish whatever work I needed to get done today.

"Sure."

"Do you need a lift home?" I asked, glancing at my watch. I needed to get moving.

"I'm fine. I called for an Uber already." She nodded and opened the door further so she could leave. "Thank you for last night. It was amazing on so many levels. I didn't know I could feel like that."

I walked across the bathroom tiles and cupped her face. "That's only the beginning, beautiful girl." I kissed her goodbye and she fled, leaving me with a raging hard-on and a head filled with excitement for what the night would bring.

12

———

AXEL

'd had one hell of a day and when I'd finally scarfed some dinner down, the last thing I'd wanted to do was get back in the car and drive out to the suburbs to pick up my date. But this wasn't just any date, it was Chastity, so I'd hauled myself into the shower, put on a fresh shirt and black jeans, and got in the car.

If it had been any other woman, I would have delayed. But instead, I pulled out my cell phone and sent a text apologizing for being late. I wanted to see her, and even after a shit day, I still wanted to. That said a lot about how much I was beginning to like her. A fact I both found amazing and wanted to ignore.

I pulled up outside a tiny little cottage about twenty minutes out of the city and sighed. I was tired of working so fucking hard every day. Success and enough money to have a comfortable life were always the goal, and now I was missing out on a lot of the "life" side of things. It was probably time to look at my business structure again. See what I could back off.

I got out of my sports car and walked up to the door, texting Chastity as I went.

58

The red door opened, and behind it stood a woman about forty.

My age.

She had shoulder-length blonde hair and lines around her eyes that spoke of stress and hard work.

"Hi. I'm—"

"Axel. Yes, I know," Chastity's mom said, interrupting me.

I grinned at her. She obviously hadn't gotten the memo that people didn't interrupt billionaires. And I liked the fact that she hadn't. "Yes, that's me."

"I'm Katherine," she said, holding the door open, but not inviting me in. "Chastity! He's here!"

I almost laughed but didn't. The tone spoke of long-suffering, though I don't know what she would have suffered with a good girl like Chastity as her daughter.

Then Katherine turned to me, her gaze narrowing in an assessing look I'd seen too often on her daughter's face. "Do I know you from somewhere?"

I looked at her again, something niggling in the back of my head as well. "I was actually going to ask you the same thing. You look familiar to me."

Katherine nodded. "Me, too. But I doubt we've ever hung out in the same circles."

I nodded and hummed in agreement. She was probably right. A single mother who hadn't gone to college. Not the type of woman I would have dated, thank God. Because that would have been awkward as hell.

There was something strangely familiar about her, though. I felt like I'd seen her before, when she was younger. Or maybe I was just confusing that thought with how much she looked like Chastity? Weird.

"Hey!" Chastity suddenly stuck her head in the doorway, her hair freshly styled and her face full of makeup.

I blinked. "Wow. I don't think I've ever seen you so done up."

Her mom growled. "That's what happens when she spends too much time at her father's. She forgets how to be a girl."

I reached out a hand to her, and she took it. "I kind of like you better natural." And I did. The makeup added years to her face. She had such beautiful, clear skin beneath the foundation. It seemed strange to me that her mother would try to hide that.

"Thanks." Chastity said, beaming up at me. "Give me two seconds." She squeezed my hand, then raced off, back into the house, leaving me standing on the doorstep with her mother. Again.

"I might wait in the car," I said, nodding to her. "It was nice to meet you."

She gave me half a smile in return. "It was nice to meet you too... and I'm sure it'll come to me when you leave where I've seen you."

"Good night," I said in return and fled to the car.

People tended to say that if you looked at the mother, that was who your woman would turn into in twenty years' time, but I wasn't sure I believed that. Katherine had an edge to her that I hoped Chastity would never develop. It spoke of heartbreak and disappointment.

When I got to the car, I turned around just in time to see Chastity kiss her mom on the cheek, and with a bag now casually hanging over her shoulder, she came running at me. I held out my arms and laughed as she jumped into them, hugging me tightly. I didn't lift my gaze to look at her mom, though I could feel the heat of her stare boring down into me. "Shall we go?" I asked.

"Yes!"

I held the door open as she climbed into the passenger side. Once I'd shut the door, I waved to her stony-faced mother and jogged around the car to get into the driver's seat.

Once inside the car I glanced at her face again, relieved to see her fresh, bright face once more. "You got rid of the makeup," I said, turning on the ignition.

She grinned. "Hell, yeah. I hate that crap."

"Then why wear it?" I asked, pulling into traffic, and sliding my hand over her bare thigh. She wore a denim mini skirt and a white tank top. Extremely causal and too sexy by half.

"Because my mom kinda makes me." She shrugged. "She likes me to dress up if we go out, and since we went out for dinner, it was expected."

I nodded, not sure how to broach that one. "Are you and your mom close?"

She sighed. "I know what you're thinking."

"No, you don't," I said, turning the car onto the main road.

"I do. You think she seems like a bit of a bitch, and I suppose to some people, she can be. But she's been a good mom."

I nodded. "That's great, I'm glad you had her. But, yeah, she does have an edge to her that I didn't expect. You're so relaxed and open."

She laughed. "That's because I'm more like my dad. You'd like him, I think. He's fit, like you. And funny. He doesn't take life too seriously."

I grinned. "Definitely sounds like my kind of guy."

And considering how old he'd be, I didn't really want to think about it. I'd always assumed my father-in-law would be at least twenty years older than me. If this relationship got to that point, that was not going to be the case.

I shook myself and took my hand off her thigh and put both hands on the steering wheel. *Fucking hell. Father-in-law? Seriously? Get your head in the game and out of the clouds.*

"So, what are we doing tonight?" Chastity asked.

"Anything you want." I said, grinning at her. "I was thinking we could have a few drinks, then back to my place maybe?"

She reached over and ran her hand over my denim clad thigh. "I think that's an awesome idea."

Blood throbbed in the lower regions of my body, and I groaned. "Now I want to pull over and ravish you in the car."

Chastity looked up and down and around the car, then sat back and laughed. "Uh... yeah... no. This car was not meant for ravishment."

I chuckled at that. I wasn't going to tell her that the seats reclined and if she got on top, I was pretty sure we could manage it. Because if I did, the cheeky girl would want to know how I knew that, and I wasn't telling the truth about that, either. "You're right," I admitted. "My bed would be a lot more comfortable." So, I focused on getting us back to my apartment.

We passed a busy area of exclusive, boutique shops and I slowed down. "There are some nice bars around here. How about we grab a cocktail or something before we go home?"

Every woman I'd ever met would have agreed to that. This part of the city was ritzy and expensive, and she would have jumped at the chance to get free drinks and be seen on my arm. I was photographed regularly around here, unfortunately, and the gold-diggers loved that sort of publicity.

So, when she screwed up her face and said, "No thank you," I was shocked. And that was an understatement.

"You sure?" I asked again.

She slid her hand over my thigh. "The only cocktail I want is in this car. Are you going to let me drink that one?"

I glanced over at her face, and she looked utterly serious.

Heading to my building, I pulled the car into my parking lot and didn't utter a word until I'd parked in my reserved spot, turned off the car and twisted around in my seat to look at her. Had she just said what I thought she said? "Um... could you repeat that please?"

Her eyes lit up with mischief before she glanced down at where her hand still lay on my thigh. "I was hoping you'd let me play with you tonight, like you did with me on Sunday night."

I swallowed hard. Part of me was excited that she wanted to play with my body at all, but another part of me didn't like the idea that she wanted to take over the evening's activities. I'd been hoping for a repeat of the other night, minus her passing out. "You'll need to be specific here," I said, licking my lips. "My imagination is spiraling out of control."

She flicked her gaze up to mine and smiled shyly. "You gave me the most incredible night, and I want to return the favor. Teach me what you like."

"So... you don't want to have sex tonight, then?" I asked. "You want to just play some more?" I was feeling totally out of my depth once again, a feeling I was beginning to uniquely pair with Chastity.

"If you don't mind waiting a little longer?" she asked, her tone hopeful. "There's no rush, is there?"

I took a long breath, then shook my head. "No, of course not."

"Good," she said, grinning now. "So, let's go upstairs and you can show me all the things you like, and what you want me to do to your body." She opened the door and hopped out of the car, but I was frozen in place.

She wanted to give to me? Since when did that happen? I shook my head and joined her in the parking lot.

We walked over to the elevator and made our way up to the penthouse, where I was about to give a lesson, I never thought I'd give. This girl was going to be the death of me, I was sure of it.

13

———

CHASTITY

I could tell I'd shocked him, which had been the plan. The man obviously didn't have enough joy in his life, and he deserved to be spoiled. I shook my head at my own thoughts. Of course, he was already spoiled. Or was, if you asked anyone with eyes. And yet, I had the feeling that he wasn't spoiled in the way I planned. I wanted to give to him and receive absolutely nothing in return other than the pure happiness that would come from seeing him fulfilled.

He'd given so selflessly to me last night, I intended to return the favor. In truth I wanted to see him lose his mind with pleasure, wanted to see him lose control. This guy had way too much control over his body, his food, his business, his life. And honestly, he seemed to lack fun despite the wealth, the women, and the toys.

The elevator took us up to his expensive apartment and as we walked into the room, my breath caught in my throat, excitement filling me up.

"A drink first?" he asked, leading me into his plush living room. "Or..."

I took his hand and tugged him towards the bedroom. "I think I choose the or option." He chuckled as he let me pull him into his bedroom and shut the door. Not that I thought anyone would walk in on us, but I wanted him to stay and not leave me. "You're going to have to tell me what you like," I said, forcing myself to speak through the nerves that closed off my throat. I had butterflies the size of elephants flapping around in my belly. "Because I literally have no idea what I'm doing."

I reached for the buttons on his fitted blue shirt and slowly began pushing them through the holes. I heard him inhale, and a similar gasp caught in my own throat. He didn't answer my question, so I didn't stop with my unbuttoning. I just kept my gaze and my focus on the buttons in front of me.

Another one popped through, then another one, revealing his gorgeous body. A body that he obviously worked very hard at, because the muscles beneath the shirt were not ordinary muscles. They were simply perfect. "God, you're a masterpiece," I whispered as the shirt slid to the floor and I was able to run my hands over his smooth, warm skin. His huge pecs, his thick arms.

He hissed as I stroked his abs, dipping my fingers into the grooves between each of his muscles. The man was so defined, he was breathtaking.

I sighed happily and enjoyed the luxury of the time he was affording me. Being able to just touch him. No rushing forward to the next step. I glanced up at him through my eyelashes and found him staring down at me. "Is this, okay?" I asked.

He jerked out a nod.

"What's wrong?" I asked, not sure if I should continue with my seduction or not.

"I have no idea what we're doing," he bit out, sounding angry.

My arms fell. "I just wanted to pleasure you."

He grabbed for me, dragging me closer against his body, and that's when I felt his erection digging into my stomach.

At least he's turned on.

"I want to take you to bed," Axel purred into my ear. "I want you to come all over me again."

I groaned. *Damn it. Why did he have to make this so difficult?*

I pulled back and stared at him. "You're not used to being told "no," are you?"

He stopped growling and grabbing at me, then his arms dropped away as though I'd offended him. "Uh..."

I took his hand in mine again and led him to the bed. "I want you to teach me everything you like. How to touch you. How to kiss you. Everything." *How to lick you and suck you,* though I couldn't say it aloud. I swallowed hard against the insecurities that rose. "Unless me being so inexperienced is a turn-off and you don't want to teach me."

"No, no, no. That's not it. I just..." Axel sighed and lifted a hand to run his fingers through his hair.

His muscles flexed and bulged with the movement, and I groaned as I wrapped my arms around his torso and pressed my lips to his bare chest. "Damn, you're gorgeous," I said against his skin, kissing him.

He sighed and cupped my face, tilting my chin so I looked up at him. "You're going to drive me to distraction. I'm not sixteen anymore." He paused, and I waited. "But if you really want to do this, Chastity... then, yeah. I can teach you."

I almost clapped with joy but restrained myself. Most likely the juvenile move would probably kill the mood.

I mock frowned at him. "Then please, get naked."

Stepping back in an obvious move to watch him, his jaw practically dropped open. I loved it. The man I'd met in the gym a few days ago had been ultra-confident about who he was and in the appeal of his body. But the man who stood before me now didn't grin or smirk. He stared at me with an intensity that made my breath catch in my throat. There was true vulnerability in his eyes, and beneath that was the man I really wanted to know.

"Please?" I whispered, begging now.

He finally moved, with sharp, jerky movements. Reaching down, he undid his belt, then unbuttoned his black jeans with a flick of his wrist. "You get naked too," he growled.

Not quite sure that was a good idea, I decided I'd meet him halfway. "Well... last night you kept your pants on." I pushed my denim skirt to the ground. My panties would stay on, but it would be amazing to be almost naked with him.

"More," he demanded, and I laughed.

So impatient.

I pulled my tank top over my head, and his eyes flared with lust. Feeling confident now, I unclipped my bra and let everything fall around me. The panties stayed on, though. There was no way I could part with them tonight. This was meant to be about his pleasure, not mine, and I was one hundred percent positive that if I took them off, we'd be going all the way.

Axel continued to stare at me, and my nipples tightened and tingled under his gaze.

I didn't cover up, though I was tempted. Everything about this man made me nervous and insecure and excited all at once. But the other night had proven to me that he found my curvy body attractive, so I flicked my hair over my shoulder and lifted my chin.

Another growl sounded, and this time I got to watch him kick out of his shoes and socks, then push his jeans to the floor and stand up again. He was as naked and as glorious as the morning I'd seen him in the shower. But this time, I wasn't running off home, I was here to devour him.

I dropped to my knees and crawled over to him on the plush carpet, wanting to pleasure him in a way I'd heard of, and even seen in X-rated movies but never actually done. When I came close to him, I pushed up and knelt before him, staring at his cock and swallowing hard. Damn, it was getting bigger by the second. I put my hands on his thighs, feeling the heat of his skin and loving the way his muscles bunched beneath my palms. "So? How do I do this?"

He groaned, the sound seeming like it had been ripped from his chest. "You don't know? You've never...?"

I shook my head. I hadn't. I'd gotten close, but most guys wanted everything or nothing, so those nights had ended more abruptly than expected.

"Oh my God." Axel moaned, covering his face with his hands.

I frowned. "If that's an issue, I can..."

He dropped his arms and one of his hands tangled in my hair, gripping the back of my head. "It's not an issue. It's too fucking hot for words."

Pleasure tightened my chest. "What do you mean?"

He sighed. "I'd like to think I'm a modern man. I accept everyone has a past and have never before been turned on by the idea of a virgin before. But knowing that this mouth—" He ran his free hand over my face, his fingers brushing my lips. "—has never been anywhere else... Fuck, I feel like a caveman with how possessive I'm feeling towards you."

I liked the sound of that. "Because you don't want me to do this to anyone else?" Hopefully my assumption was on target.

He didn't answer, he just shook his head.

Good. I didn't want to do this with anyone else either, though I knew he didn't want to hear those words. We had no commitment to each other and on a rational level, I knew that I would have another lover after Axel. Probably more than one. But in this moment of perfection, Axel was mine. And I was his. And I didn't want to think about tomorrow.

He grabbed his shaft and held it in his hand. "The head is the most sensitive part. It's the same cells that your clit is made from. So, concentrate on that part with your lips and tongue."

I nodded and leaned forward, pressing a kiss to the big, bulbous head. It was so much warmer and smoother than I thought it would be. Opening my lips, I pulled the head into my mouth, licking it and sucking at it, trying not to use my teeth.

Axel's hand was still in my hair, but he wasn't moving me or guiding me in any way.

I rocked backwards and looked up. "Is this okay?"

He nodded, his face flushed with heat. "You can use your hands too, if you want."

As I nodded, he let go of himself, reaching for my hands and guiding me up to grip his shaft. "Just... suck the head, and move your hands up and down."

I did as he said, gripping the thick shaft that was getting thicker by the minute, loving the feel of the softness of the skin. Silk over steel. I moved my hands up and down, having down that part before, then sucked on the head again. Damn, this was hot. But what else could I do for him?

I began to explore him a little more, running one hand down his thigh and up again, venturing between his legs to softly cup his balls and stroke through his legs to cup his ass. So many places to kiss. Once again, I pulled off and glanced up at him. "Can you lie down? I want to do more."

14

AXEL

More? She wanted to do more? She was fucking killing me. Slowly, deliciously, killing me with that mouth of hers. And she wanted to do more? "Um, sure. Where do you want me?"

"Lie down on the bed."

Fucking hell. I turned around, crawled onto my bed—my domain, my pleasure sanctum—and lay on my back. Then I waited. Seriously, what was going on around here?

"Do you have any lube?" she asked suddenly, popping up next to me on the bed, her gorgeous boobs bouncing enticingly.

"Yeah. Top drawer," I said, pointing to the nightstand.

She hurried across the bed, pulled open the drawer, grabbed a tube then crawled back over, a huge grin on her face.

"Lube, huh?" I asked, lifting an eyebrow. "I thought you were a virgin."

She giggled. "Um... I go to college and have an iPhone. I've seen porn and have friends who are quite experienced and don't hesitate to talk about it. So, I know what goes where."

And from the look of her, she was trying to explore everything in one night.

"Well, I'm all yours," I said, putting my arms behind my head and relaxing into the pillows.

"Brilliant." Dropping the lube on the mattress, she swung her leg over my waist so that she was on top of me.

"Now we're talking," I said, grabbing her waist and thrusting up against her. She still wore her panties, but I was pretty sure I could talk her into taking those off.

Before I even had the chance to touch her, she shimmied down to lie down on top of me and kissed my lips.

I kissed her back but then she was gone, kissing down my neck and licking my nipples. "Oh, you don't have to do any of that." I didn't really like extra attention on me. It made me feel a bit... strange.

She glanced up at me, then narrowed her eyes. "You don't like it? Are your nipples sensitive?"

I shook my head. "No, not really."

She shrugged and put her head back down, flicking my nipples with her tongue and her nails, and causing sparks of pleasure to twirl inside my gut. That wasn't something I was used to. Then she sucked on one of them, and I gasped.

She looked up and grinned. "Just let me enjoy myself. It's my turn." She kissed all the way down my stomach, then pushed my legs up so that my knees were bent. What the hell was she going to do now?

"Have you done ass stuff before?" she asked, kissing my cock and nuzzling into my thighs.

"Some. Why?" Did she really want to know about other women I'd had anal sex with? That really wasn't necessary, was it?

She nodded and began to nibble and suck the flesh on the insides of my thighs. Then she was touching me with her fingers, probing my ass.

"What are you doing?" I asked, looking down at her, my eyebrows halfway up my forehead.

She was kneeling now, squirting lube onto her fingers. "Ass stuff," she said simply. "You said you've done it before."

Holy shit! That wasn't exactly what crossed my mind when she'd asked about anal play.

But then she grinned, showing so much enthusiasm for what she was about to do, there was no way I was going to say no. "There's something I want to try. Is that okay?"

I nodded. "Yeah, of course, but..."

She bent her head and sucked the sensitive head of my cock into her mouth.

I groaned and clenched the sheets beside me. *You've gotta be fucking kidding me!* I was already too turned on. Her tenderness, sweetness and enthusiasm for my body were going to get me off too quickly.

Then her fingers began slipping between my cheeks, circling my asshole and pressing in.

"Oh, God." I groaned, sitting up, only to have her push me down with her free hand.

I grabbed onto her arm, needing an anchor of sorts. Suddenly things were unstable, the mattress felt like it was moving and shaking beneath me.

She sucked me and fondled me, then moved her finger in and out of my ass, sending wave upon wave of pleasure through my body.

"Fuck... I..." I couldn't talk.

Chastity never stopped. She pleasured me and attended to me like I was her sole focus.

My orgasm began to tingle at the back of my legs, and I forced myself to take deep breaths, slowing down my breathing.

But she didn't let me separate myself from what we were doing, and I didn't get a moments rest from the exquisite torture. She just kept sucking and licking and pleasuring me in ways no one had ever done before, which if I were honest, was one of the biggest turn-ons about her.

"Chastity... You've gotta stop." And she did. I was about to come in her mouth, and that wasn't something I wanted. Not for her, or me.

I wanted her closer, wanted her lips on mine.

"No."

I growled when she wouldn't stop. Sitting up, I grabbed her and hauled her up onto my body.

"I want to make you come." She pouted.

"Oh, you will," I gasped out. In fact... I rolled her over, so I lay between her legs, my aching cock pressed against her pussy. I grinded against her. "I want inside you so badly," I said, dropping down so that I was speaking directly into her ear.

"Can you come like this?" she whispered back.

I groaned. "Hell, yes. But you've gotta fuck me back."

She wrapped her arms and legs around me, arching up into me as I drove against her again and again, only one thin piece of cotton separating my cock from her pussy. She gasped and groaned and clung to me in a way that made me want her so much more.

My orgasm flared in my gut and this time I wasn't fighting it. The heat tingled up my back and roared down my thighs. My balls tightened and I thrust into the cradle of her hips one more time.

She turned her head and said in my ear, "I can't wait to feel you come."

And I lost it. I cried out like an animal, shooting my seed all over Chastity's panties and belly.

She held me through it, her fingers digging into my back and her heels digging into my ass, holding me as tightly as she could against her.

For me, the orgasm was one of those that go down in history as the longest, loudest, most drawn-out of pleasures. I couldn't stop the groans that flew from my mouth, nor the way I shuddered as my cock pulsed and spasmed between us.

When she turned her head towards me, I captured her lips with mine, partly to stop the noises that fell from me, but mostly because I wanted to kiss her more than anything in the world right now.

The blazing hot pleasure began to recede, and a wash of shame pushed at me. I should never have let her seduce me like that. At the very least she deserved an orgasm of her own. I pulled back to stare down at her, her cheeks flushed and hot with arousal. "Next time we come together."

She giggled and nodded. "Absolutely. But I have to say, that was fucking hot. We can do that anytime." She smiled up at me with so much pleasure that any feelings of regret began to recede.

Rolling onto my side next to her, I ran a hand over her sticky belly. "How about a shower? And I can make you happy with my fingers this time?"

She rolled onto her side to face me. "Yes, to the shower, but I'd rather wait for my next orgasm, if that's okay."

"Why?"

She shrugged her elegant shoulders. "Because this night is all about you. That's what *I* want."

I shook my head. "You don't make sense."

She sighed. "Look, I know you're used to being in charge, and giving everyone else everything they need."

I narrowed my eyes at her. "You don't know me well enough to say that."

She tilted her head to the side. "Am I wrong?"

I stilled, thinking about her words then realizing that for a woman who'd only known me a few days, she seemed to understand me better than people who'd known me for decades.

"No. You're not wrong."

She smiled softly. "Then let me spoil you. Let me pleasure you and expect nothing in return, just for one night. Because I know once we start having sex, we'll never be able to go back to these nights of amazing foreplay, will we?"

I chuckled. "No, I don't believe we will." I didn't want to admit it aloud, but I was pretty sure that her pussy was going to be as addictive and enticing as the rest of her. Glancing at the clock across the room I realized it was almost midnight. "So... what should we do? Showers, then take you home?" I didn't really want to let her go, but we hadn't discussed tomorrow yet.

She sat up and swung her legs off the bed. "Definitely showers, but I was hoping I could stay again. Then I'll Uber back to Mom's in the morning."

"Did you bring anything to stay?" I asked, getting to my feet as well despite the lethargy that tugged at me. *Damn, I could pass out this very minute.*

She grinned. "Yep. Toothbrush and clothes for tomorrow are in my bag."

I shook my head. *I've never met a girl who packed so light.* "Then you're set," I said, thinking about the guest bedroom that waited for me down the hall. I'd lie with her until she fell asleep and if I was still awake, I'd go to my own bed then.

"Shower time," she said, then my gaze caught on the clock next to the bed. One minute after midnight.

It was officially tomorrow, which meant it was *my* turn again.

15

AXEL

followed Chastity into the ensuite, loving the way her generous ass swayed as she moved. She was all curves, and she was absolutely gorgeous. I flicked on the water and adjusted it so that it was soon steaming hot, and she moved beneath the spray. She was naturally, gloriously beautiful. Bright eyes, amazing smile, perfect skin. And her body was so inviting I couldn't wait to touch her again.

I watched her quickly rinse off, then when she turned around to smile at me, I moved in. My hands ached to touch her, and they weren't going to be denied. If she wanted to wait to have sex then I'd wait, but that was where following her lead ended.

I cupped her face and kissed her, stepping into the shower, and feeling the hot water washing over my face and body. She grabbed my waist and held me close, kissing me back with all the passion and need I'd hoped for.

My hands roamed her body, loving the smoothness of her back and the indentation of her tiny waist. I cupped her breasts because moving past them without touching them was impossible. Those fleshy globes were soft and full and filled my hands perfectly.

She moaned, arching back to give me better access.

I pulled away slightly, nibbling on her earlobe and whispering to her, "It's tomorrow, you know. It's not your turn anymore."

She gasped but pressed closer. "I don't want to—"

"I know you don't," I interrupted. "But you aren't going to sleep with that deep ache between your legs."

She moaned softly and thrust her hips against mine, my cock beginning to rouse once again. Poor bastard didn't know that sex wasn't on the menu tonight.

"You do ache for me, don't you?" I asked, loving the way her small hands grabbed for me, keeping me as close as possible to her.

There were no games with this girl. She didn't try to play hard to get or demand I jump through a hundred hoops to get into bed with her. She was panting and needy, and I wanted to give her the relief she deserved.

"Yes, I do," she said, moaning into my ear as I slid my hands down to her ass and pulled her tight against me.

"Then it's time for another orgasm. *Yours*," I said, pressing her back against the cold tiles and hearing her gasp once more. I tilted the shower head so that she had hot water pouring over her and she stared up at me, quivering with the dual temperatures. "Do you want me to?" I asked, wanting her consent for everything I was about to do to her.

She nodded. "Yes. How are you going to manage that here?"

My brain threw images at me of lifting Chastity up against the tiled wall and thrusting my cock up into her waiting pussy again and again until she cried out with ecstasy. I shook myself. That wasn't the plan for tonight. I grinned at her. "Open your legs and I'll show you."

She nodded, her thighs falling open as she leaned back against the tiles, her chest heaving with arousal.

"Damn, you are the hottest woman I have ever known. How do you do it?" I demanded as I stepped closer.

She huffed out a laugh. "What are you talking about? I'm a mess."

I didn't know how to explain to her that her inexperience, her enthusiasm, and her beauty were an intoxicating combination. I bent my head to kiss her, and she wrapped her arms around my neck. My tongue slid into her mouth, tasting her sweetness as I moved my palm over her belly and ran my fingers over her mons.

"Oh, shit," she gasped out. "I want you so much, it's insane."

"Tell me more," I demanded, sliding my fingers over her swollen clit and parting the slippery folds.

"I... uh... want you inside me so bad..." Anything more eloquent seemed to fail her at that point.

I groaned at those words, finding her slick entry and sliding two fingers inside her pussy.

She clamped down at me, squeezing my fingers tightly.

"God. You're so perfect." I captured her lips with mine and there were no more words, only moans and groans. Gasps and cries of pleasure.

My fingers worked her body, making her climb higher and higher. And when she finally came apart in my arms, shattering into a million pieces, a part of me knew I would never be the same again.

"Bedtime?" I asked her when her shuddering had subsided and she was slumped against me, her head resting on my shoulder.

She nodded. "Yes, please."

Turning the shower off, I grabbed towels from the rack. "Here you go, beautiful." I wrapped the towel around her, and she sluggishly moved towards the bedroom once more.

"You okay?" I asked, chuckling at the way she staggered and stumbled like a drunkard.

She giggled as she dried herself, then flung the towel over the chair next to the bed. "I feel amazing. Drunk, but better." She pulled back the covers and climbed into the bed, crawling to the middle of the mattress and laying on the pillow as close to my side as possible. She reached out her arm and patted my side. "Come. Please."

I crawled into bed and lay down, facing her. "Sweet dreams, sweetheart."

She reached out, under the blankets and lay her hand on my arm. "Thank you for tonight. It was amazing."

I grinned at her. "It certainly was."

She nodded and closed her eyes, her little hand curled around my bicep.

I watched her fall asleep and everything in me was content. Happy. More than I'd been in so long, I couldn't even remember the last time I'd felt anything like it. Even with the women and the money. I closed my eyes and let myself relax into the pillow.

I'd had a shit day at work, and a brilliant session with her, but I was never going to be able to fall asleep. As soon as I closed my eyes, my subconscious would percolate up everything I worried about. And the downward spiral would begin. I began to pull away, determined to sleep in the room I reserved for these nights.

"Don't go," she whispered. "Cuddle with me." She rolled over, pushing her ass back into the cradle of my hips and nestling into me like a cat.

"I'll stay for a while," I said, sliding my arm over her waist and holding her close to me. I could think about work while I lay here. I didn't really need to go anywhere. "Sweet dreams, Chastity."

She sighed happily and I closed my eyes again. She was warm, and soft. Inviting in a way that women who were too skinny just weren't. I was beginning to think that my taste in women was changing.

The software company merger... I tried thinking about the deal I had on the table, but my brain wouldn't grab onto any of the facts, and I slipped into sleep.

16

AXEL

*W*aking up with her in my arms again was startling. She was so hot and soft, draped all over me. I felt instantly over-whelmed and suffocated, though my stomach lurched at the idea of kicking her out so that I could get ready for work. I moved away from her and took a breath. This was too strange, too different. *How is this even possible?*

"Good morning," she said to me, rolling onto her back and stretching her arms above her head. The sheet slipped down to her waist, exposing her gorgeous, pink-tipped breasts.

My mood changed instantly, my half hard cock rousing to full mast. "You sure you don't want to change your mind about the timing of your next step?" I asked, running my hand over her tight nipples.

Chastity giggled. "Don't you have work this morning?"

I did. I always had work to do. "It can wait."

She laughed louder this time. "Yeah, right." She rolled out of bed and grabbed for her bag, pulling out the clean underwear she'd packed yesterday.

I sat up in bed and watched her get dressed, loving how free and relaxed she was. There was no darting to the bathroom to put on makeup, no covering up or turning away. It was almost too relaxed, too easy. And I didn't trust it.

"When are we catching up again?" I called out as she pulled on a simple sundress and started tying up her shoes. Damn, this girl did not mess around. I'd struggle to get ready so quickly.

She pulled out a hair elastic from her bag and swept her long blonde hair up into a ponytail. "I don't know. What sort of schedule do you have this week?"

"Terrible." I groaned. "Meetings every day, but I'm sure I can squeeze in another late date one night." Maybe. I had plans to wine and dine some international visitors, and some of my meetings would go into the early hours of morning.

"How about I pop by for lunch sometime this week?" she suggested, grabbing up her bag.

"Sure, but when are you going to stay over again?" I asked.

Chastity grinned. "I'm spending a few days with my mom and have plans with friends, since I only have a few weeks off. But how's the weekend for you?"

I frowned. "I have a party Friday night, but we could catch up after?"

She bit her lip. "I have plans Friday night too, not sure how late it'll be. Are you free Saturday night?"

I didn't really like the idea of waiting five days to see her again, but this week would fly with all the work I had to do. "I can clear the weekend for you." I said with a grin. Once I got her into my bed, I wasn't letting her out again for at least two days.

She walked over to where I lay on the bed and leaned over to kiss me sweetly, then pulled back with a smile. "I better get going. Thank you again for a great night."

"Have a great week with your friends," I managed to say, though the words sounded like sawdust in my mouth. *Fuck it.* I was jealous of anyone who got to spend time with her. What was wrong with me? I raised a hand and waved at her as she walked to the door. I was starting to think she was opposed to breakfast the way she kept running off. "See you on Saturday."

She grinned at me as she headed out the door. "Bye."

And with that, I flopped back on the mattress and covered my face with my hands. I had it bad. And unlike most of the women I dated, whose appeal lessened with every date, my attraction to Chastity was only growing. I sighed and hauled myself out of bed and headed for the shower. Why did I get the feeling that no matter how much time I spent with Chastity, I was never going to get sick of her smile?

17

CHASTITY

The plans I'd made with my mom suddenly seemed lackluster compared to what I would have been doing with Axel.

"What are you thinking about?" my mother asked me, looking over her expensive cappuccino. "You look a million miles away."

I picked up the little silver teapot in front of me and poured myself peppermint tea. "I don't know…"

"It's Axel, isn't it?" Mom asked, sighing heavily.

I rolled my eyes, immediately annoyed at her. "Why do you have to say it like that?"

"Honey, you're about to finish college and head off to chiropractor school. The last thing you need is to start some *relationship* that's never going to last."

I took a sip of my tea, though my stomach dropped with a lurch. Why did she have to be like that? "Why won't it last?" I asked, though I didn't want to know what she thought.

Mom had dated a few guys since she and Dad had divorced, but never been serious with any of them. Things just always "didn't work out" and I often wondered if it was them, or if she had some issues that she simply couldn't get past.

Mom sighed again. "Sweetheart, he's twice your age."

"And?" I said, annoyed that his age was the first and only argument Mom had with me. "I love how old he is. How smart and successful and fit he is. Guys my age are skinny, lazy, and horny, and just..." I shuddered. "Gross." They also weren't into serious relationships. They all wanted to screw around for a few years before they settled down, so a virgin like me was a red flag for all of them.

"Then find someone five or even ten years older," Mom said with a sigh. "Not twenty. People will think you've got daddy issues."

"Mom!" I groaned and pushed my half-eaten chocolate croissant away. She'd just ruined my appetite.

"It's true, Chastity."

"Well people can think what they like. I do not have *daddy issues* because I've always had my dad. He never abandoned me, never moved away, never stopped loving me." I huffed at her. No matter how many times she liked to complain about my dad, I wasn't disappointed in him. "He never got re-married, never had any kids..."

"Neither did I!" Mom defended.

I glared at her. "And I don't have any mommy issues either, so stop trying to put your shit on me."

My mother's eyebrows flicked up. "What's wrong with you tonight?"

"Nothing!" I said, annoyed now even though I was the one who had ramped up the fight. "I just... I like him, Mom. A lot. And I don't want you shading me or him when I've never even dated someone before. You just can't do it." I was so agitated, my arms were shaking, so I stuffed my hands into my lap and squeezed my hands into fists.

"Okay, okay. Chastity don't blow a gasket. Geez."

I stood up abruptly, afraid I'd start yelling if I stayed with her a moment longer. "I'm just going to the bathroom. Won't be long." I snatched up my cell phone, went to the ladies' room and sat down in a stall. I didn't need to go, but I needed a moment to myself, a second to breathe. I got my phone out and decided to message Axel. After all, why not?

Hey! How's your day been?

I sent it off, then decided to cruise Facebook for a minute before going out to brave my mom again. God, she could be such a drag. If I wanted someone to give me hope or support or love, she wasn't the one I went to. And that was kind of sad.

Hey, yourself. Day was busy but good. How about you?

I couldn't stop the immediate flush of happiness that permeated every cell in my being at his response. I giggled to myself, not caring if someone heard me and thought I was crazy.

Good overall. Mom's being a pain in the ass.

I bit my lip and waited for the response.

You okay?

Again, my heart took flight. Damn it, I was *sooo* into this guy.

Yeah, no problem. Just tired, I think.

I could almost hear his chuckle in my ear. He knew why I was tired.

We had a late night and an early start.

No regrets.

LOL. Never.

I wished I had a photo of him just so I could look at it for a minute. Definitely something I'd have to do next time we were together. And speaking of which.

I haven't got any plans for lunch tomorrow. Where will you be around 12? 1? Can we catch up?

He didn't respond right away, so I got up, left the stall, and washed my hands. I'd organized to catch up with some friends tomorrow, but I could push them back to the afternoon. My heart wouldn't be happy until I saw him again.

I could probably take half an hour off around 1pm. Though, can I confirm tomorrow? Meetings change last minute sometimes.

I dried my hands and picked up my cell once more.

Yeah, sounds great. Text me the address and I'll be there.

He did, sending me the address of a building right in the heart of the city. If Mom wouldn't lend me her car, I'd just take an Uber. Wouldn't be too expensive, hopefully.

I took a deep breath before heading out of the bathroom and walking back to the table.

"You're smiling again, that's good," Mom noted, still eating her grilled chicken salad.

"Yeah, everything's fine. Are you almost ready to go home, Mom?"

"Oh?" Her tone was filled with disappointment. "I was hoping we could stay out for a bit. Go for a walk. Catch a movie. Something."

I tried not to grimace visibly. "I'm starting to get a real headache mom. Can I take you out for breakfast instead? My treat."

Mom lit up at the idea of another meal out. I had money saved, and I had no issue spending everything on my mom. She and I might clash a bit, but in the end, I owed her for my life.

"Okay, sweetheart. Let's go home and put you to bed."

Mom tucked me up and took me home, and I curled into my tiny single bed and dreamt of the king size bed I'd slept in the night before.

THE NEXT DAY I took Mom out for brunch, had a long shower, braided my hair, and got dressed into some of my best clothes. Proper black pants, nice sweater. I was going into the city to meet Axel in his work environment. A denim mini skirt and flip flops would not cut it, I was certain.

I even tucked my long braids up into an elaborate design at the back of my head. I looked thirty. Maybe. I put on mascara and a rose-pink lip gloss and was ready to go. "You sure it's okay if I take your car?" I asked my mother as I grabbed the keys and packed my bag.

. . .

"Of course, hon. You won't be long, right?" Mom asked, walking out into the hallway. "Wow. You look nice. Where did you say you were going again?"

I didn't.

"Meeting Axel for lunch," I said with a brilliant smile and turned away with a wave before she could say something cutting about my extremely hot, pseudo-boyfriend. I didn't really know what to call him. "Bye, Mom!"

I ran to her car, got in, and started it. It had been ages since I'd driven a car since I didn't have one at school. I just didn't use it enough to justify the expense. I drove the half an hour into the city, hating the traffic and the inability to find parking, but at the same time, I couldn't be annoyed. I was so freaking excited to finally see him.

Luckily, I found a lot with a few spots open a block from Axel's building. I had about fifteen minutes to walk to his address, so I sent him a message.

Just parked. Will walk over and meet you where? Lobby? Outside?

I was almost at his building when the message came back.

I'm running a little late, so come up to the office and I'll order us in some food.

I wasn't going to argue with that. I arrived at the address and my mouth fell open. It was a fucking skyscraper! "Whoa." *Please let him have some little dinky office on the third floor.* Because the idea of facing the reality that Axel really was as rich as he claimed was finally sinking in. *He's a billionaire. A billionaire. Say it again.* "A billionaire," I whispered to myself as I stepped into the lobby and went straight up to the reception desk.

"Can I help you?" the smartly dressed woman behind the sleek desk asked.

"Yes, I'm here to see Axel Patterson. He said to come up to his office."

The woman smiled back. "Yes, Mr. Patterson said he was expecting someone. Go right over to those elevators. Forty-second floor."

"Forty-two?" I repeated, aghast. That was a little too high in the sky for me.

"Yes."

She returned to answer the phone and I headed over to the elevator and got in. "Holy shit," I squeaked to myself as the doors closed and I rode all the way up to Axel's floor. When the elevator doors dinged open, I was greeted by another reception desk. "Um, hello," I said to the woman behind this desk who looked about sixty and seemed like the kind of professional who should be running her own business.

"Can I help you?" she asked, staring down her nose at me.

"I'm here to meet Axel Patterson for lunch," I managed to say, standing tall and straight, and trying not to fidget.

The woman looked me up and down, and I wasn't sure she liked what she saw.

"Don't worry," I whispered to her, because I couldn't help but attempt to make her smile. "My mom doesn't like the fact I'm dating him either."

The old crone actually cracked a smile and walked around the desk. "Let me show you to his desk personally."

I didn't know why that sounded like a huge compliment, but I flashed the woman my brightest smile, and was led down an imposing, long hallway until finally I stood before two large, impressive doors.

The receptionist, who was probably the office manager, knocked and I heard Axel's annoyed voice call out, "I'm rather busy!"

I giggled and covered my mouth with my hand.

"Your name, dear?"

"Chastity."

The woman's eyes lit up with amusement. "Shall I send Chastity away, sir?"

There wasn't a verbal reply, instead, the door opened abruptly. "No. No, Cheryl. Thank you."

The office manager winked at me and walked away.

Axel turned to me with an awestruck look on his face. "How did you get that dragon to like you?"

I laughed, "By not treating her like a dragon, for one thing." I grinned at him and despite my better judgement, jumped at him and wrapped my arms around his neck. "Hey, you."

"Hey, yourself," he growled, and whisked me into his office, the door shutting loudly behind us.

AXEL

kicked the door shut, the sound reverberating through the empty room. Then the little vixen moaned, and my cock swelled against my suit pants. Damn it. I could take her on the desk this minute if our relationship was at that point. So instead of lamenting the loss of the great sex that could happen, I put all my energy into the kiss. I thrust my tongue deeply into her mouth, tasting her sweetness and exulting in the groans that erupted from her throat.

She felt so good, a refuge in the storm of the day I'd had. Grabbing her ass, I kissed her hard, and for a few minutes I couldn't think of anything but her. It was bliss. When she finally pulled away, the euphoria eyes made me smile. "Hey."

"Hey," she said as she cupped my face and smiled.

Something strange winged through my heart at the look in her eyes. Was this what it felt like to be in love? To want someone in every part of your life, not just your bed? She'd already wrapped my dragon of an office manager around her little finger, and I could see myself meeting her for lunches and dinners, taking her home to meet my parents.

Holy hell. Slow the fuck down. I grabbed her wrist and pulled her hand off my face, suddenly irked by all the thoughts pulsing through my brain. "I ordered lunch. It should be here soon," I said, taking her hand and drawing her over to the leather couch against the wall.

She didn't sit down, instead disentangling our fingers and walking over to the window behind my desk. "Holy shit!" she gasped. "This view is insane!"

I shrugged. "Yeah, I guess so."

This has been my office for almost ten years now. I'd slowly but surely taken up more and more of the office building and the upper twenty floors were all my employees now.

She spun around. "And this office! Axel, you could play volleyball in here!"

I glanced across the expanse of my workspace and tried to see it how she did. To me, the large desk, visitors' chairs, bookcase, and couch were just props designed for ease of work and to impress people who walked in for a meeting. It seemed like she was impressed, which I supposed was the point.

"Not an activity I've considered," I told her seriously. Volleyball? I hadn't even looked at a net since college. And back then, I only played on the beach so that I could show off my upper body. That usually guaranteed me a woman or two in my bed that night. I hadn't had much back then.

She came back to my side and sat down on the couch. "So, what's for lunch?" She was all bright-eyed and bushy-tailed.

I tried to lift myself up to her level of excitement—but failed for some reason. Perhaps I was starting to worry if all my money and success were a major factor in her wanting to date me. "It'll be here in a moment." And as if my words had conjured the delivery, there was a loud knock at the door. "Come in!" I called out, and a young woman walked in with tray full of food from the restaurant downstairs.

"Hello, sir," she said with a polite bob of her head.

"Just put it all on the table," I requested, reaching for Chastity's hand.

But she jumped up and went over to the server, giving her a beautiful smile. "What did you bring us?"

The server glanced at me, then looked back at Chastity. "Well, there's a bit of everything for lunch. Both tuna and chicken salad in tomatoes, roast beef sandwiches with herbed cream cheese, cucumbers and greens, soup and fresh baked rolls with homemade butter."

"Sounds delicious. Thank you," Chastity said to her, and the woman all but lit up with her smile.

"Yes. Thank you," I added, realizing that I really didn't think twice about the people who worked for me, and how much like me they were.

The girl left and Chastity started uncovering all the dishes. "How's your day been, Axel?"

I leaned back against the couch and watched her taking in the spread before us with excitement.

"Honestly?" I asked.

"Yep. If you're having a shit day, you can tell me. You don't have to answer with the standard 'good.'"

I laughed. "Well, yeah, it's been shit. A merger I've been working on for a month is looking like it won't go through, and I've put in too many hours on it to lose now."

"Do you want a selection?" she asked, picking up one of the plates to start dishing out. "Or do you want to come choose?"

"A bit of everything is fine." I answered, not feeling hungry. I didn't eat well when I was stressed.

But she made us up two plates, then came and sat down next to me with a sigh. "This looks so good. Thank you."

She picked up half of one of the roast beef sandwiches and ate it with a moan.

My heart kicked out at me again. She was happy. Truly happy just to sit here with me, eating takeout from disposable containers with no one around to see us. Was it expensive takeout? Yes. Was my office a million-dollar space, yes? But perhaps that wasn't the reason for her happiness. If that were true, she would be truly unique.

"Enough about me. What about you?" I asked her, picking up one of the tuna-filled tomatoes and taking a forkful.

"I'm fine." she said. "Had breakfast with Mom this morning and catching up with some high school friends for dinner."

"Busy girl," I said with a grin.

She giggled. "Yeah, well, even though school isn't very far, I don't really hang out with anyone during the semester. I study hard and socialize when I can, but I generally wait until the holidays to really catch up with everyone."

I nodded, my memory casting me back to my college days. "One long party, right? College? Your weekends must be full."

She shrugged. "Not really."

I stared at her, not seeing any signs that she was lying. Damn, the girl was an enigma.

"You and your mother, okay?" I asked, "I got the vibe from your messages last night that you two weren't getting along well."

She tilted her head to the side and kept munching, and that's when I noticed how corporate she looked. Her hair was all tied up so I could barely see it, and she was covered from head to toe.

I frowned at the black pants. Nope. They didn't suit her or her laid back personality, either.

"We're okay," she said, "We're always okay. She raised me, so I don't think I'll ever let go of the feeling that I owe her for my life, but at the same time, we're very different, so we butt heads on occasion."

"And you butted heads over me?" I could imagine that to a protective mother, a guy my age wouldn't look like the best prospect for her daughter.

She shrugged again. "Yeah, we did. I like you, and she thinks there's no future for us because you're so much older than me."

I opened my mouth to respond then slammed it shut again. *Whoa. That was a bit too intense for me.*

She laughed at me. "You look like I just proposed marriage or something. Relax. I just told Mom that we're having fun. I'm only here for a few weeks, anyway."

I nodded. "That's true."

Her statements made me feel better on some level, but they also tugged at my gut. I only had a couple of weeks with her before she headed off for her last semester before chiropractic school and possibly started a career in another state.

"Speaking of our limited timeframe, what did we agree to this weekend? Are we catching up Friday night?"

She looked out the corner of her eye at me and waggled her eyebrows. "Anxious to get into my pants, are you?"

I glanced down at the black slacks she wore. "Not these ones, I can tell you. Where are your normal clothes? Your dresses and skirts."

She raised an eyebrow. "What's wrong with my outfit?"

"It's so..." *Boring, conservative, old.* "Not you. I like how you usually dress."

She sighed. "And my hair?"

Hated it.

"It's pretty," I hedged. "But can you take it down?"

"You prefer it like that?" she asked, as though wanting to confirm my reasoning behind my statements.

I nodded. "Hell, yes. Can you take it down?"

She stared at me for a moment then nodded. She tilted her head forward, then painstakingly took out a dozen or more hair pins, which loosened the braids that fell, then she started to unwind them. "I thought you might like me looking a bit older. More mature. I was trying to fit in with your co-workers, so you weren't embarrassed by me."

I outright laughed at that one. "I don't want you to fit in, sweetheart, you were born to stand out."

She poked her tongue out at me for that one. "That is so cliché."

And the fact she didn't fall for cheesy lines like that made me like her even more. "Remind me again when you're sleeping over?"

She ran her fingers through her long blonde tresses then looked at me. "Better?"

I reached over and tangled my fingers in the strands, then cupped her head and dragged her mouth to mine. "Much better."

We kissed again, and this time I kissed her slowly, exploring her lips and inhaling her scent.

When we finally broke apart, my pants were tight once again. "So?" I asked, still nose to nose with her. "Friday night?"

She nodded. "Okay. After my family thing."

Oh, damn, I'd forgotten about my best mate's party. "Okay." I'd leave early if I had to. Patrick only turned forty-two once, sure, but having sex with a girl like this? It was a rare gift.

We finished our lunch and then I had to get back to work.

She left and I spent the rest of the day on a high, not allowing the people around me to stress me out like they normally would. I had a date to look forward to, and at this moment in time, it felt like the most important date in the world. Friday night.

19

CHASTITY

The next two days flew by quickly. I kept myself busy as I normally would, and messaged Axel any chance I got. He was always flirty and thoughtful, and it made me ache to see him again. But his workload was kicking his ass, so I convinced myself that it was better if I simply stayed busy and didn't try to sneak in an extra visit. The nights of kissing, orgasms and fun and foreplay were amazing for me. The best "almost sex" I'd ever had.

But from Axel's point of view, I was beginning to think that he was getting frustrated not being able to go all the way, which was expected really, considering he was a man who'd done it a thousand times. Probably more. It would be like telling a professional football player, "yeah you can play the game you love, but just until halftime, then you've gotta get off the field and go home."

But soon that would all change. He would make love to me, and my world would forever be different. I'd no longer be a virgin. And after waiting so long for the right person, it felt incredible to say that I'd found him.

"You ready to go?" My mom asked as she stuck her head in my room, wearing her robe and slippers.

It was finally Friday night, and I had my dad's faux-fortieth birthday party to attend, then I'd be heading out afterwards to meet Axel. He'd actually turned forty, two years ago, but thanks to a global pandemic that had us all avoiding parties like the plague, he was making up for it tonight.

"Yeah, I think so." I said, checking myself in the mirror one more time. I was an hour late because the hairdresser I'd gone to this afternoon had been running way behind and I'd taken way too long to get ready.

"Your dad's gonna have kittens over that dress," my mother said, giving me a visual once-over, though her smile said she liked the idea of my father being annoyed at me.

"It's the second anniversary of his fortieth birthday," I justified. "I have to look nice." And the fact that I'd bought a brand-new dress, and expensive underwear had nothing to do with the fact that I was meeting up with Axel later. *Nothing whatsoever.*

"You sure you don't want me to drive you?" Mom asked for the tenth time.

"Yeah. I'm sure. Though I can't wait to get my own car." In a few years when I had the money, and hopefully would have the time to drive around, I'd buy my own car.

"Well, have a good night," Mom said, her sadness eating at me.

I knew she wanted to come with me, but there was a toxic nature to my parents' divorce that I'd never quite gotten to the bottom of. Neither of them had ever re-married or had more kids, which made me think that perhaps they were destined to get back together. But then again, that was probably just some childish fantasy I held onto and shouldn't.

"You too, Mom. I love you."

"I love you too!"

My phone beeped. Uber was here. "Gotta go." I grabbed my jacket, covered up all the bare skin I was showing, and raced to my Uber. This dress was mid-thigh, skin-tight, and had spaghetti straps that barely kept it up. It was hot. And it was nothing like the clothes I would normally wear. But tonight was special. Tonight, I wanted to feel beautiful.

Dad's place was only twenty minutes away, and while I jiggled nervously in my seat, I messaged Axel but didn't get a response. He said he had to do something tonight. A friend's party, or something. I didn't know. And it didn't really matter, we were catching up at a club in the city tonight, then I'd go home with him. I just had to get through the family stuff first.

When we arrived, I paid and jumped out, grateful for the fact that I hadn't driven. The place was packed. It was Friday night and there were cars everywhere. I ran up to Dad's apartment and knocked on the door. A moment later the door flew open.

"Auntie Shell!" I flew at my dad's sister with my arms opened wide.

She laughed in my ear and hugged me back. "Oh my God, you are so gorgeous. Let me look at you."

We pulled apart and she held my hands, opening my arms wide. "You are freaking gorgeous! When did that happen?"

I laughed, knowing she didn't mean any offense. "I think you're being fooled by a nice dress and some makeup, Auntie Shell."

She smiled at me with a familiar grin. "You haven't lost your down-to-earth sensibility. I'm so glad." She shut the door behind me and took my coat. "I'm putting everyone's stuff on your father's bed. When you're ready to leave, you can grab it."

"Thank you! Do you know where Dad is?"

She waved her hand in the air. "In the middle of the fray. You know what he's like."

I grinned. I sure did. My dad was extroverted and single, which meant he had a lot of friends, and from all walks of life. There would be people here from his work, his gym, his high school. He collected people and they stayed around forever, something I loved about my father.

I walked down the short hallway, grinning as the music began to pound through my chest. When I stepped into his large living room, there were people everywhere. Food was laid out in platters on the kitchen counters and some heads turned to look at me as I stepped forward. One head in particular. "Axel?"

It looked like he was mid-sentence when he stopped talking to a couple of guys and turned to look at me. His gaze raked me from heels to lips, and back again.

My belly tightened and heat coursed through me. He was seriously the most breathtaking man in the world to me. That smile... damn, the things I'd do to have him smile like that at me.

He said something to the people to whom he was speaking then walked over to me, a beer in one hand.

"What are you doing here?" he asked, leaning forward to kiss me.

I knew my dad had to be around here somewhere, so I dodged his lips and quickly kissed him on the cheek, but damn that was hard! He wore dark wash denim jeans and a fitted white shirt and looked just... fucking hot. There was no other way to put it. He looked lean and powerful, and I suddenly wished he could throw me over his shoulder and take me with him this very minute.

"Me?" I asked, giving him the same look he was giving me. "What are you doing here?"

"Chastity!" My dad yelled out, barreling across the room to grab me up into a hug, the scent of wine and whiskey wafting around him.

I laughed as he lifted me up, then put me down. "Happy birthday, Dad."

Axel's eyes goggled out of his head. "Did you just say *Dad?*"

I nodded. "Yeah, why?"

Axel glanced away, his jaw tight and angry.

"What's wrong?"

Dad put an arm around me. "Hey, sweetie, how do you know this big lug?"

"Ah..." Well, shit "I don't really. We, uh... met briefly the other week when you dumped me at that expensive gym of yours for an hour or so."

"I didn't dump you," my father corrected, rolling his eyes. "But I didn't realize you two had met."

"I didn't realize you two knew each other," I added, my throat tight and hot. I swallowed hard to push back the feelings of rising panic. "Are you two gym buddies?"

The expression on Axel's face was devastated, there was no other word for it. He looked ready to commit some sort of felony. "No," Axel said, gruffly. "We've known each other for years."

"Yeah, Axel's been my best friend for at least a decade, I can't believe you two have never met before."

"I've seen photos," Axel said, shaking his head, "But didn't connect the two."

I raised my gaze to his, pain shattering around my heart. "Yeah, he probably showed you some school pictures. I don't really look like that now."

Axel looked as if he tried to smile but it came out more of a grimace.

"Speaking of how you look... jeez, Chastity, you're more beautiful than any of the other women in this room. You know you're not supposed to show everyone else up if you can help it." He winked at me, and I tried to smile but I wasn't sure if I succeeded or not.

"Don't know if that's a compliment or not, Dad," I said, elbowing him in the ribs. "But thanks. I... uh... was going to meet up with someone after the party, so got dressed up for a date." My eyes met Axel's and for a moment I saw the burning lust I'd been hoping for, then he looked away.

"Well, he's one lucky guy," Dad said. "Hey, there's some kids here your age on the balcony if you wanna go chat with them. You don't need to talk to us old guys all night, you know."

I could almost see the knife Dad had skewered into Axel's heart. "Thanks, Dad, but I think I'll go catch up with some of the family. I haven't seen Aunt Shelly in years."

"You do that, beautiful. You know how proud we are of you. Did I tell you my girl got into chiropractic school?" my dad bragged to his best mate—Axel. *My date.* What a fucking mess.

Axel shook his head. "Nope, but that's probably not your fault. I don't always listen well."

Dad *tsked* good-naturedly. "Well, bachelors don't. Anyway, see you later, sweetie." And my father turned his back on me, dragging Axel away.

I stared after him, everything in me aching yet numb at the same time. What did this mean? Would Axel want to continue this two-week fling we planned, or had the fact that my dad was Axel's best friend truly fucked up any chances of us being together?

20

AXEL

"Hey, Patrick, gotta take a leak. I'll be back."

"Use my ensuite, if you want."

I nodded my thanks. "Yep, will do." I needed some space and some time to think before my head exploded. What the hell was I going to do now? The bathroom was through Pat's bedroom, so I walked around the bed and headed to the bathroom. I used the toilet, washed my hands and checked my phone.

One text from Chastity.

I'm in an Uber, headed to my dad's birthday, and omg I am so excited about tonight! What time do you want me to meet you?

I wanted to slap myself upside the head.

How did I not know? Well, how could I have known? "Her mother! That's where I know her from."

Pat had shown me photos of his ex-wife a few times. They hadn't really stuck in my mind too much, but when I'd seen Chastity's mom, Katherine. "Kaiti, he calls her Kaiti." Something about her had been familiar. And this was why. I texted Chastity back.

Um… you still wanna meet up?

I headed out of the bedroom, suddenly afraid that she'd come and find me and then we'd get totally busted. Patrick would have an absolute fucking conniption. At least I hadn't screwed his daughter yet... but damn, had I gotten close. And damn, did I want to. Even now.

What was with that dress? And her hair. She looked amazing tonight and had already admitted to her father that she'd dressed up for her date. *Our* date. *Her dad. Fuck!* I raced back to the safety of the gym crew, where they were talking about protein shakes and what shares were up at the moment. Boring, normal shit that soothed me a fraction.

I ran my hand through my hair, my nerves shot to shit. I needed to break it off. Tell Chastity that there is no way we could meet up tonight. And we certainly couldn't get into bed together again.

"You okay, Axel?" Danny, another guy from the gym, asked me.

"Yeah. Sorry, just had a big week." I managed to have another beer and found a spot in the corner, sitting at the table chatting with some friends who didn't need me to carry the conversation because I sure as hell couldn't talk like normal. My brain was ninety percent consumed with the girl who was currently flitting around the apartment as though nothing was wrong.

Chastity was talking to everyone, hugging anyone who came towards her, and serving food. The lady of the house. Her gaze occasionally caught mine, but then one of us would look away and the spell would be broken.

"Is that Pat's daughter?" Danny asked suddenly, pouring himself another whiskey.

"Which one?" I asked.

Danny grinned at me. "The one you haven't stopped staring at all night."

I looked properly at Danny this time. I'd never thought about him being that insightful or clever, but from the grin on his face, I wasn't going to be able to bullshit my way out of this one.

"Yeah, that's her," I admitted.

"She's beautiful," Danny said solemnly.

"Yeah," I managed to say, taking another sip of my drink.

"Do you know her?"

I stared at him for a minute, not sure how to answer. I didn't want anything getting back to Pat, but at the same time, damn, I could use a friend.

"Yeah... we met a few weeks ago. I didn't know she was Pat's daughter."

"And you two..."

I shook my head. "No. We just shared a few meals."

I'd gotten as physically close as possible to fucking her as someone could get without actually doing it. But Danny wasn't getting the details. No one was.

"So, what's the problem?" Danny asked.

"The problem..." I moved closer so the people around us wouldn't hear. "The problem is that I was hoping to meet up with her again. But I can't now. And that's fucked."

"Why not?"

"Why not?" I repeated, incredulously. "Because Pat would fucking kill me if he found out. She's his only kid. And she's..."

"What? Half your age?"

I growled at him. "Fuck you."

Danny laughed. "Look buddy, I've known you a long time. If she's special, and you think you could make it work long-term, go for it. But if you just want another toy in your bed, then yeah, let her go." He shrugged like it was that easy.

And, yeah, it probably was. My phone vibrated and I picked it up.

Yeah. I still want to meet. At the club like we planned? Or somewhere else?

I glanced around but Chastity was nowhere to be seen.

We can still go to the club, but how about you walk down to the cafe on the corner, and I'll pick you up and drive you.

It was risky. Someone could see her getting into my car, but I didn't want her to order a ride. We needed to talk.

When I looked up from my phone, Danny was staring at me. "You like this girl, huh?"

I ran a frazzled hand through my hair. "Yeah, I do." My phone vibrated again.

I've got my coat. Give me five to say goodbye and I'll meet you down the street.

I glanced up and saw her re-enter the room, all smiles as she hugged her dad and said goodbye to his family. She was just as beautiful as the moment I'd met her. All bright vivaciousness. Natural charisma.

When she headed out the door I glanced at my phone. "I'd better go. My car is parked at the far end of guest parking." It wasn't. I'd gotten a spot not far away, but I needed to go.

Danny held out his hand. "Nice seeing you, man."

"Yeah, you, too."

"Don't tell me you're leaving as well!" Pat said, coming up to give me a hug.

I hugged him back. "Happy Birthday, Patrick. but yeah. Got some late conference calls with Taiwan. Gotta head out." I hated lying to him, but the truth was gonna sting a lot worse.

"Cool. See you Sunday morning for a run?"

"Yes," I told him. It wasn't like I had plans with Chastity anymore. "See you then."

Patrick headed off, and I practically ran for the stairs. My heart was pounding now. I was excited. I could feel the edges of my mouth tick up. *Shit! No! You're going to break up with her. Don't get all excited to see her.* I tried to dampen down my enthusiasm as I ran down the stairs, found my car and drove to the end of the street.

But there she was, waiting for me, her black coat covering her gorgeous dress, and her long blonde hair flowing down her back. She turned at my approach and for once, her face didn't light up when she saw me. Instead, she simply nodded, walked over, opened the door, and got inside.

As soon as her seatbelt was on, I drove off, getting into the lane to hit the freeway, and the city. "You still want to go to the club?" I asked her.

She nodded. "Yeah. I want to dance. With you. Just once."

She sounded so sad I reached over the space between us and grabbed her hand with mine. "You okay?"

She twisted around to glare at me. "No! I'm not! This night was meant to be..." She growled and shook her head. Then she crossed her arms over her chest, effectively dislodging my hand.

I put both hands back on the steering wheel, pain in my gut now. She was upset. "Tonight was meant to be what?" I knew, but it felt like she needed to say it.

"Tonight..." She took a deep breath. "I thought we... Let's not talk about it. Let's just go and have a drink, and a dance, and—"

"And what?" I asked. "Say goodbye forever?"

She stared out the window. "We have to. There's no other way, is there?"

I gripped the steering wheel until my hands ached. We didn't talk for the rest of the drive, and I pulled into the closest valet parking. When I turned the ignition off, she unbuckled her belt and got out of the car without waiting for me to get her door.

I took a steadying breath. *You can do this.* I got out of the car, locked it, and handed the keys over to the valet driver. When I reached for her hand, she came to me, gripping my fingers and pressing into my side as we walked up to the front of the club.

"Do you think we could forget about my dad, just for an hour?" she asked. "I just want to enjoy *us* for a little bit more."

She sounded so depressed, I tugged her into my arms. "The world isn't ending, sweetheart."

She nodded then blinked, tears soon cascading down her cheeks.

Oh, crap. I kissed her quickly, unsure how to otherwise stop her crying.

She cupped my face, then wove her fingers into my hair, holding me tightly against her.

My cock throbbed and I pulled back. If we started fooling around, I was done for. There was no way I'd remember why we couldn't be together if she started touching me. "Let's go."

I knew the bouncer at the club, so he nodded at me as we approached and opened the door for us.

"Ohh, fancy," Chastity said as she went ahead of me.

I bit back my retort. I had more money than I knew what to do with, and no one to spend it on or enjoy it with. I could give this girl the world, if she wasn't the only person I couldn't have. And for the first time in my entire life, a saying that my friends had used all the time rang through my head: *"Sucks to be me."*

21

CHASTITY

I wanted to cry. I'd been holding it in all night, pretending to be happy and social. Filling the void of the wife-figure my dad didn't have. I'd served drinks and food, pandered to my aunts and uncles. And all I wanted to really do was bury myself in Axel's arms and cry my eyes out. But now that I had him all to myself for a very limited time, the last thing I should do was cry. I wanted to dance.

The music was great, playing some sort of deep-base techno with no words. Just a great vibe, dark lighting, and bars aplenty. I stopped walking and Axel slid up behind me, his lips at my ear and his hand around my waist, holding me close.

"Do you want a drink?"

I nodded and turned my head towards him so that our lips were only a few inches apart. "I think I need one."

"Me, too," he growled back, and pushed his hand into the small of my back. "Let's go to the bar."

I let him lead me through the throng of hot people pressed against each other. The music was so loud I was going to need to holler to be heard, and then I wouldn't be able to speak tomorrow. Or we could just not talk. What more was there to say, really?

Axel was my father's best friend. Dad would be horrified to know that I'd jumped into bed with him. And even if I could get over the link between them, there was Axel. I'd seen the look on his face. It was like he was suddenly disgusted by me. My age. Who I was to him now. His best friend's daughter.

He'd known all along how old I was and yet, there was nothing like realizing he was literally older than my father to put a damper on things.

"What do you want?" Axel shouted next to my ear.

"Something strong."

He leaned over the bar and spoke to the bartender.

A minute later, two shots of tequila and lime slices were lined up in front of me, and another two were lined up in front of Axel.

He turned to me, a shot held in the air, waiting for me to join him in drinking away our sorrows.

I picked one of mine up and we clinked them together.

He threw his back and grabbed the slice of lime to suck on, gasping as the gasoline-like quality of the straight alcohol hit him.

I did the same thing, wincing as the burn traveled all the way down my throat to my empty stomach. I'd barely eaten all night. The first shot down, I picked up the second.

Axel nodded and once again, we clanked our little shot glasses together and tipped back the fiery liquid.

As I gasped and sucked on the lime wedge, I wondered what we were toasting. The end of our relationship? Getting this far and finding out just in the nick of time that we really, really shouldn't be together?

"Thanks!" I yelled at him, already feeling the warmth of the liquor moving through my veins.

"Let's dance." He took my hand and led me to the dance floor.

Women stared at him as he walked past them, one girl practically falling over herself to come and speak to him.

I just gaped at her arrogance, whereas he shrugged her off with a tight, annoyed grimace.

Then he pulled me into his arms and everything in the world was right again, if only for tonight.

I put my arms around his neck and moved to the music, smiling and laughing as he grinned down at me.

The music changed into something faster, and I was shocked when he moved back and began to move his hips like a pro.

I put my arms up in the air and let the music take me.

We danced and laughed our way through so many songs I lost count. Until the tequila had made my head fuzzy and my heart sing, and my mind was struggling to come up with a reason we shouldn't do this every night.

I moved closer to Axel and wrapped my arms around his neck. Then I went up on my toes and lifted my face to be kissed.

He didn't hesitate, wrapping me in the tightest hug and kissing me until I was seeing stars.

When he lifted his head, I whispered. "Take me home. Please."

The cloud of lust that had been enveloping us seemed to vanish in a single moment. Axel lifted his head higher, further away from me. Then he gently but firmly pulled my arms from his neck and back down to where they came from.

"We need to talk. Come on." He grabbed my hand and pulled me through the crowd, towards a door at the back of the club.

"Where are we going?"

The enormous bouncer who stood at the door had a lethal expression on his face. But the moment he saw Axel, he stepped aside and opened the door for him.

"Ummm..." *Where are we going now?*

"Come on." Axel tugged me through the door, and up a flight of stairs.

My legs were not steady, and by the time we got to the final step, I almost stumbled. In fact, I would have fallen ass over tits in my very new and expensive dress if Axel hadn't swept me up into his arms.

"You, missy, are drunk," he growled at me, like it was my fault.

"Yeah, whatever." I wasn't impressed that he wanted to blame all this on me.

"Whatever?" he repeated, his eyebrows raising in surprise.

"Yeah. Whatever." I said again, flicking my hand dismissively. "I didn't eat at my dad's, and you know why. And then you gave me shots on an empty stomach."

He plonked me down on an empty couch, and that's when I glanced around. "Where are we? Some sort of private bar?" I couldn't see the club from here, but I could hear the music.

There were couches and tables around, but no one else in the space.

"Yeah. It's for VIPs."

I bit the retort that came out my lips at that. Was there anywhere he didn't go? Anyone he didn't know?

As though in answer to my thoughts, an older guy reeking of whiskey stumbled by.

He straightened when he saw Axel, then tugged on his jacket as though that would help his appearance.

"Axel. Haven't seen you around here for a while. What have you been up to, man?"

Axel's lips tightened and he held out his hand to me.

I didn't hesitate, I moved straight onto the couch next to him and he put his arm possessively around me.

"Not much." Axel said nonchalantly. "Work. Nothing new."

The guy unbuttoned his jacket and slid onto the couch I'd just been occupying. "This a new one?" he asked, nodding at me.

Axel stiffened beside me. "This one... is none of your business."

I couldn't read the room well, so kept my mouth shut. Their relationship seemed strange. Strained, as though they'd once been friends, but not anymore.

The man, whose name I still didn't know, laughed. "You mean this one isn't for sharing? Come on Axel, she looks hot."

He licked his lips and let his gaze roam over me like he had the right to look at me like that.

I shuddered and turned my whole body into Axel.

Axel's growl was almost feral as he reached across the small divide and grabbed the other guy by the tie, then hauled him off the couch.

"Get out of here," he snarled at the drunk. "Or I'll have you thrown out."

He tossed the guy to the side, then slid back onto the couch with me.

The asshole got to his feet and stuck his nose in the air. "No need to be so fucking pissy. If this one is special, you just needed to—"

"Sam!" Axel called, and out of nowhere, a huge, bald bodyguard appeared. Axel flicked his head in the idiot's direction, and he was escorted from the room by the bouncer.

I nestled closer to Axel, my heart hammering in my chest. "That guy was creepy."

Axel put his arm back around me and grunted. "He was a good man, once upon a time. We went to college together."

"What happened to him?"

Axel tightened his hold on me. "Divorce, business failure, normal shit. He's an alcoholic now, and a miserable bastard. I can't believe he got in here."

"Why?" I looked up. "Because this place really is for very important persons only?"

He crushed his mouth to mine, and I slipped my tongue between his lips, needing to get closer, to taste him. To be a part of him.

When he pulled back from the kiss, he sighed. "I would have killed him if he'd touched you." He pressed his forehead to mine.

"You mean you didn't want to share me with him?" I joked.

Axel grabbed me around the waist and hauled me over his body, so I was straddling him, my dress up around my ass, exposing my thighs and my underwear to him.

"Is that a 'no'?" I asked, breathless.

Axel ran his hands up the outsides of my thighs and stared up at me. "No. I would never share you. With anyone."

His words were clipped. Short. As though he were still angry.

I slid closer to him, pressing my panties against the crotch of his jeans. "Why won't you take me home, Axel?" Surely, he wasn't planning on having sex with me for the first time up here? It was nice, but privacy was definitely a problem.

He groaned and dug his fingers into my thighs. "Because if I take you home, I'll fuck you... and that's not on the table anymore."

Even though I knew it, hearing it come straight from Axel's lips made my heart sink. I'd been so close to getting what I wanted.

"I know," I said, slumping.

Then I glanced up and met his eyes again. "Do you think we could just have one night, tonight, then pretend we've never met?"

Axel stared at me for a long, intense moment. Then he shook his head.

I groaned like an impatient toddler. "Why not?"

He sighed. "Because I couldn't just let you out of my bed after one night, Chastity. I just know it. I'll want you over and over again."

My pussy throbbed at the mention of all the sex I would have been getting if it weren't for the fact that my father knew Axel first.

"This is so not fair," I pouted, running my hands over his broad chest. "How well do you know Dad? I mean, is he just a friend you see once a year?"

"I have a key to his apartment."

Oh, fuck. I thought I was the only one except for my father's cleaning lady who had a key to his apartment.

"He loves you," I whispered.

He nodded. "And he loves you."

Tears gathered in my eyes, hot and horrible. "So essentially, we're fucked."

He pressed his lips into a thin line. "I think we'll break his heart and his trust if he finds out we're doing something like this behind his back."

Did we have to sneak around behind his back? Probably. Since this relationship was only destined to survive a few weeks at best, I couldn't exactly come out and say, "Hey, Dad, we're just fucking each other while I'm on summer break. Don't stress about it.'

"Is that what you want?" Axel asked, because I'd obviously been silent too long.

I shook my head, the tears were now falling down my cheeks. To hide them, I fell into Axel's arms and buried my face in his neck.

2 2

CHASTITY

The next day, I couldn't get out of bed. Just waking up hurt.

"Hey, sweetie! It's almost noon. You wanna go out for lunch?" Mom called through my closed door.

"No, thanks!" I called back. "But I'll get up soon." Then I pulled the comforter, quite literally, back over my head.

After we'd decided that it was probably best to quit while we were ahead, Axel drove me back to my mom's place. Neither of us had wanted to say goodbye, so instead we'd just held hands for a few minutes, then I'd gotten out of the car and run for my life. I didn't look back because my face was covered in tears, and I knew that Axel felt bad enough as it was. We'd made the right decision, but fucking hell, it was a bastard of a choice.

Then I'd officially had the worst night's sleep of my life, or at least in my memory anyway. Mom always said I'd been a terrible sleeper as a baby. It had taken me hours to fall asleep, then I'd been haunted by nightmares that had woken me up multiple times before I'd finally passed out from exhaustion after sunrise.

My head kept circling back to one universal truth. *It wasn't fair.* I'd waited patiently for the right guy to come along, for the man I

115

finally wanted to fall into bed with, and I'd found him. The fact that he was my dad's best friend shouldn't have mattered, should it? But it did. I knew it did. It only highlighted our age gap, and how different our lives were.

Not to mention the fact that my father would be horrified. And although I was pretty sure that no matter what I did, I wouldn't lose my dad's love or our relationship, I was pretty sure Axel would lose his. I didn't want to do that to either of them. Not for the sake of a relationship that wouldn't last.

Of course, part of me wanted to yell that it could last forever if we both wanted it to work. But that was just the teenage version of myself talking. That tiny part of me that still believed in *happily ever after*. And love at first sight.

But I had to face facts. Axel had never said anything about a long-term relationship. If anything, he'd made it clear it wasn't on the table. And I was leaving for school soon too, so the likelihood of being able to make "us" last was minimal.

I sighed and pushed the comforter back off my hot face. It was lunchtime. I needed to get up and go out. Make some plans. I'd deliberately kept this weekend free for Axel. So that we could spend as much time together as possible, if we wanted to. Now I had days and days of nothing to do, except maybe getting ready for Christmas.

That thought got me moving, and I quickly jumped in the shower and got dressed. "Hey, Mom! Wanna go into town and do some Christmas shopping?"

"Sure," she called back, sounding happy at the invitation.

I tugged on a hoodie, not caring what I looked like today. "Great. Let's go."

2 3

AXEL

Sunday morning.

I pulled on my joggers when I heard a knock at the door. "Coming!"

When I got there, I pulled the door open, a part of me secretly hoping it was Chastity. Damn, I missed her. "Oh, hey, Patrick."

"What's wrong with you?" Pat asked, handing me a blue Gatorade. "Hung over?"

He pushed past me into my apartment, and I groaned. *Thank God Chastity isn't here.*

"We were supposed to go jogging. Sorry man."

Patrick and I went running most weekends. He was a great training partner, fit and determined.

"All good," he said, cracking open his drink and taking a swig. "I ran here, so I figured you might wanna join me for a bit."

I definitely did. Something had to get me out of this funk. "Give me two minutes." I walked to my bedroom and pulled on some socks and shoes, then went in search of a tank that wouldn't irritate me while I ran.

"Hey," Pat called from the doorway. "You okay?"

"Yeah, why?"

He shrugged. "Don't know. You were a bit odd on Friday night, and now... I don't know. Just wanted to ask. Check in on you, because I know not many dare to ask." He grinned at me to show he was joking.

I sighed and ran my hand through my hair. "Yeah. I..." How much could I tell my best friend? "I started dating this girl a week or so ago."

"Oh, yeah? She screwing with your head already?" Patrick laughed.

My gut tightened. "Yeah, she is. But it's... I don't know. I like her. I just don't know if I can do anything about it."

"Hang on a second," Pat said, putting his hand up. "You actually like this girl? Since when do you get attached?"

I got to my feet and pulled on a thin, cotton white tank. "She's different."

Patrick laughed at me again. "And by that, do you mean she's a brunette rather than the normal blonde?"

I groaned and scrubbed my hands over my face. "You really think I'm a shallow asshole, don't you?" Which boded even worse for me if Chastity and I decided to date. Pat would never want me, with my history, anywhere near his daughter.

Patrick sobered instantly. "Hey, man, I didn't mean to offend you. It's just... hey, if you actually like her, I'm happy for you. I just never thought you'd find someone worth settling down for."

I grinned at him. "I didn't say that." Settling down was another chapter entirely. Then I shrugged and stood up. "I just like her."

"Then go for it," Patrick said, walking forward and clapping me on the back. "Any woman who has you distracted, forgetting your schedule, and tied up in knots must be worth chasing after. I've known you for ten years and never seen you like this."

I nodded my head, my heart sinking. "Yeah... maybe. You're definitely right about that run, though. I could really use a heavy training session."

"Let's go, then." Patrick put his Gatorade down on the table and dumped his keys and cell phone. "Can I leave all my shit here?"

"Yeah, of course. We'll just take a key." I left my cell phone in my room, just in case Chastity called or texted. She hadn't since Friday night, but it would just be our luck that the one time she did, her father would see it.

Once I'd stashed any potential evidence of Chastity away, we headed out. We took the elevator down, then started stretching and began our run. We jogged through the city and made it all the way to the beach. By the time we got there, I'd developed a good sweat, and my heart was pounding.

"Oh, yeah. That feels better," I said, bending forward with my hands on my hips and breathing deeply.

"So, where'd you go Friday night?" Patrick asked in between panting breaths. "You said you had a conference call, but I know you. Did you catch up with the chick you're hung up about?"

I nodded. "Yeah. Went to Chase's. But we pretty much ended it before it began. She's... too different. Young."

Patrick chuckled. "Half your luck, bro. Let's go."

We turned and headed back, running around each other, and sprinting along each street.

When we finally got back to my apartment, my legs were shaking. "Fuck, that was good."

Patrick nodded, red-faced and completely out of breath.

I went straight for the fridge, where I pulled out a couple of bottles of water and tossed one at him. "You got plans for Christmas next week?"

Patrick nodded, drinking the water and lifting his tank to wipe away the sweat on his red face. "Yeah. Meeting my parents for lunch and having my daughter over for dinner."

My stomach lurched and I turned away to get something to eat. "You want some eggs or something?"

"Nah, I've gotta get back, actually. Got a date myself, for lunch."

I turned and stared hard at him. "A Sunday afternoon date? Who are you, and what have you done with my friend?"

Pat had been pretty burned by Chastity's mom, and I'd never known him to date anyone seriously.

He laughed at me. "Pot. Kettle."

"Touché."

"Maybe we're just getting too old," he joked.

That is very possible. I'm kind of sick of waking up alone.

He walked over and held out his hand. "Thanks for the run, Axel. You should get strung up over a woman more often. I haven't had that good a run in ages."

I slapped him on the shoulder. "You enjoy your lunch date. I hope she ties you up in knots."

Patrick huffed and headed out, whistling softly.

Wow. He actually sounds pretty happy. I shook my head, scrambled up half a dozen eggs, then dug into them. Damn, I was hungry. Then it was shower time. I was sweating from the back of my neck to the soles of my feet. I scrubbed myself hard and let my mind wander to work. The Taiwan merger. Employees to hire and fire. A new building I wanted to buy. Anything and everything. I let my mind whirl.

But by the time I was dressed again and about to turn on my laptop, my brain was back on Chastity. I reached for my phone. We hadn't made any rules about our supposedly ended relationship, so a text wasn't off the table.

Hey. What are you up to for Christmas?

I put the phone down and tried to get back to work, but the device immediately buzzed with her reply. I groaned and closed my laptop, giving up. I walked back into my bedroom, lay down on the bed and opened the phone.

Hey. Mom's for lunch. Dad's for dinner. Small. Casual. What are you up to?

I smiled as I texted.

Not much. My parents are in Europe.

A moment later she responded.

You're an only child too?

I sighed and rolled onto my side. We really hadn't got into a lot of personal stuff. I felt like I knew her well, but we'd missed so many of the pedantic details that made up the person.

Yep.

I closed my eyes as I laid my head on the pillow. I hadn't been sleeping great since I "broke up" with Chastity, which wasn't unusual for me. I rarely got more than four hours sleep most nights anyway. It was the only way I'd managed to get my company off the ground. I did two eight-hour shifts every day, sometimes more.

But thanks to the few nights Chastity had spent in my bed, my body was aching for that feeling of a full six to eight hours of sleep. It had been heaven. I put my phone down next to me, forcing myself to relax. My thumbs had been poised for the next message, anxious for her. I wanted to see her. But I'd been the one to put a stop to everything.

My phone dinged.

I miss you. This is shit.

I chuckled and rolled onto my back. That was the perfect message to receive.

I miss you too. And I agree.

I hit send before I could stop myself. I could safely say I'd never felt this way before— about anyone. Perhaps it was the fact that she was untouchable? I didn't really know. But she hadn't been untouchable a few days ago, and I'd still wanted her more than I've ever wanted any woman before.

I've only got about ten days left until I go back to school full time. Are you sure you don't want to catch up?

When that message came through, every part of me sang out with happiness. She knew that this relationship wasn't going to last, and yet she wanted it anyway. I inhaled sharply and took my time as I messaged her back. After writing the response then re-writing it twice, I was satisfied.

I'd love to catch up with you. Are you sure you'll be okay to just walk away after our two weeks are done?

When I sent it, my gut tightened. I didn't want her to say no, and worrying about losing her was something I thought I'd never feel. It was a really foreign sensation. My phone vibrated straight away.

I'd rather spend two weeks with you than a lifetime without you.

"Fuck," I groaned out loud. "This girl is going to be the death of me." I typed back quickly, before I could change my mind.

My place. Tonight. eight o'clock.

I sat up on the edge of my bed as I waited for her response. When it came, I practically whooped.

See you then. xox

2 4

CHASTITY

I didn't even bother with underwear this time. I wore a maxi cotton dress that was tight around my boobs, so I didn't need a bra. It was also long enough that no one would ever know I was commando, even though it felt ridiculously naughty to be running through the city with the fresh air blowing between my legs.

I reached Axel's apartment that he owned, shaking my head. Who owned a *whole* building? I went straight up the elevator and stepped into his apartment.

"Hello, beautiful," Axel greeted me, standing in the foyer wearing a basic white t-shirt and a ripped pair of jeans. The soft fabric of his shirt clung enticingly to his muscled chest and biceps. His hair was styled, and his easy smile made him look like he should have been gracing the front of a billboard somewhere.

I dropped my purse and ran straight at him.

He swept me up against his hard body, so I wrapped my arms around his neck and hugged him tight. God, it felt good to be with him again.

When he drew back, I didn't let him speak. I just grabbed his face and kissed him deeply, wanting him to make me feel good again. My chest had felt like it had been clamped in a vise for the past forty-eight hours, and now that I was with him, I could finally breathe again.

He kissed me hard, forcing my lips apart even as his hands roamed my body greedily. He grabbed my ass and squeezed. Then he stopped kissing me and pulled back. "Are you wearing underwear?"

"No." I wore my new, expensive stuff Friday night and everything went to hell, so..." I shrugged.

His smile was too sexy for the health of my fragile heart.

He pulled further back, took my hand, and led me to the bedroom. "So... what? You figured that if you were naked underneath your dress, I could just take you against a wall or something?"

I shrugged. "A girl can only hope." And I'd definitely dreamt of that exact scenario.

He sighed as he drew me closer and cupped my face with both hands. Gently. Carefully. "Not this time, sweetheart."

I put my hands around his waist. "But maybe another time?" I asked, hopeful. I had so many fantasies I wanted to fulfil in the short time we had together. *Sex in the shower. Sex outside. Sex in a car.*

Me on top, him on top. Up against the wall. Maybe on the couch... the kitchen counter...

He chuckled. "What's going on in that amazing brain of yours?"

I smiled. "You don't want to know."

"I doubt that." He smiled. "But for now, I'll let you keep your secrets. I have a feeling they'll destroy what I have planned for tonight, otherwise."

"What do you have planned?" I leaned forward to kiss him softly again. I loved his lips. They were just so soft, full, and lush. I could kiss him all day and never get tired of his taste. His smell.

"The perfect night," he whispered against my mouth. "Where you come on me over and over and over again."

I inhaled deeply, my breath caught in my throat. I wanted that too. "Okay."

He reached down and grabbed my dress, scrunching it up so that the material slid up my legs, over my knees and up my thighs.

I leaned back and held up my arms. I smiled at him, confident and content to let him undress me. He wanted me, I knew that. From what he'd said, he wanted to get me naked from the first moment we'd met.

He lifted the dress to my waist then gave it a couple more tugs to get it over my breasts, my shoulders, then finally I was as naked as the day I was born. Axel was staring at me with ferociously hungry eyes.

"I hope you're going to get naked too." I bit my lip to stop the squeal that rose. For a single moment, I wanted to lift my hands and cover myself up. But I also wanted to drop to my knees and open Axel's jeans and take his cock out. Maybe that's the direction I'd take. I dropped to the plush carpet and reached for his jeans.

"I wasn't planning on getting naked just yet."

I tugged at his belt and flicked open the button, not wanting to give him any reason to try and escape me tonight. "I know I was the one to beg you to go slowly. And I've regretted that move a hundred times since last week." A million times was more like it. If I'd just let him fuck me the first time he'd wanted to, by the time we'd worked out that Axel knew my dad, it would have been too late.

Axel reached down and cupped my chin. "I've actually loved taking it slowly with you. It's been a unique experience."

Well, that was one good thing, I supposed. But tonight wasn't for slow. I pulled down the zipper on his jeans, slowly. His cock was already rock-hard and thick behind the fly, and as I finally got the last of the zip down and peeled back the denim, he sprang out to meet me. "Oh, hello," I said, laughing a little.

Axel reached over his shoulder and tugged his shirt off. Then he stepped back a little and pushed his jeans from his hips and strolled back to me completely naked now. "Yeah, well you're hot. I'm never *not* hard around you."

I wrapped my hand around his shaft and kissed the head, loving on him just the way he'd taught me.

He sighed and slid his hand around my head, gently guiding me as I took his cock into my mouth and went deeper.

I tasted him and explored him, his moans of pleasure echoing in the fancy bedroom until he grabbed me under the arms and hauled me to my feet.

"That's enough for now."

He reached over and stripped the blankets from the bed, then pointed towards the mattress. "Lie on your back. It's my turn to love on you."

I didn't stop to examine that sentence. Instead, I raced onto the bed, flipped over and lay with my head on the pillow.

He prowled up the mattress until he was hovering above me.

He rocked his hips against me and growled. "Damn, you're divine. I wanna take you so much."

"So, take me," I invited, spreading my legs open and running my hands up his arms.

He shook his head gruffly. "No. Not until you're begging me to."

I smiled at him. "I'll beg you right now."

He shook his head again, then this time he rolled onto his side and slid his fingers between my thighs.

I gasped as he rubbed his fingertip against my clit, startling me. "Oh!" I grabbed his shoulders, and he buried his head in my neck.

"I want you to scream for me."

I closed my eyes to better enjoy the sensations. Axel nibbled on my earlobe, then sucked on the skin of my neck. I didn't care if he gave me a hickey. In fact, I hoped he did. I wanted something to remember this moment, forever.

He moved lower, suckling at my breasts, causing arrows of pleasure to shoot through my belly.

I arched my back and threaded my fingers through his thick hair, holding him close. My eyes were closed, but I forced them open so that I could watch him.

The sight of him kissing my flesh, tugging at my nipple with his teeth was driving me crazy. There was something so erotic about seeing the real-life picture. When he moved lower, I opened my legs willingly, wanting him to do all the magical things he'd done to me the other night, again and again.

He kissed my stomach, then slid down so his head was right between my thighs. He got onto his elbows, teasing my drenched opening with his fingers.

I covered my face with my hands, arching into his caress again, then moaning loudly as he slid his fingers inside of me. "Ahhh!"

"Are you okay?"

I dropped my hands away from my face and nodded. "Yes. It's just... I..."

He moved his fingers in and out of my body, then set his lips to my clit and licked my most sensitive place.

"Holy shit!" I sat bolt upright and grabbed his hair, then collapsed back onto the bed as he began to play me like I was a musical instrument once more.

He flicked my clit with his tongue and lips, making my belly tighten, and strangled screams erupt from my throat. He stretched me with his fingers, making me crave him even more as he slid them inside of me, over and over again.

I panted and grabbed for him, then cried out as he withdrew and crawled back up my body. "Not without me this time."

"No!" I agreed, grabbing onto his brawny arms and pulling him towards me. "Please. I want to feel you inside of me."

I was empty and aching now. I'd been so close to coming, which he must have known.

Axel rolled to the side, grabbed his cock and rubbed himself against my entrance.

I moaned and tilted my hips up to him, wanting to capture his hardness and drag him inside me.

Axel rolled back on top of me and nudged the head inside of me.

I cried out, lifting my legs and wrapping my thighs around his waist. "Please." Begging wasn't beyond me at this point. I dug my heels into his back. "I need more."

He groaned as he settled over me, our lips only a breath apart. He stared into my eyes as he slid into me, an inch at a time.

I gasped at the strangeness of the feeling, then lifted my head and our lips met.

He ground down on my mouth, thrusting his tongue inside as he surged into me fully.

A spike of pain made me gasp against his mouth, but it was nowhere near what I'd expected.

He lifted his head, staring down at me with intense, lust-drugged eyes. "Fuck. You feel amazing. Like a dream."

I ran my hands up and down his arms, feeling a little strange. Awkward. "Is this it?"

He chuckled, a lightness entering his eyes. "We're just getting started, beautiful."

And then he began to move, the true dance beginning.

Every time he withdrew, I dug my nails into his flesh, wanting him closer. Then he'd surge back, and I'd moan, my pleasure ricocheting up a notch. On it went, and with every thrust of his hips, every kiss of his lips, my belly tightened.

My pleasure began to mount, and bit my lip, feeling my pussy squeezing him with every thrust he made. "I'm..." I swallowed hard, "I'm..."

He began to move faster, harder, fucking me into the mattress and making my pleasure climb higher than any peak I'd ever encountered. I went past Everest. I was in the stratosphere.

"Come on, baby," he groaned into my ear, and with that final thrust, my orgasm crested and blew apart.

I screamed, and he fucked me harder, making the wave surge higher and higher until I couldn't hear, couldn't think. I could only feel him shuddering over me, filling me with heat. Then I was falling down, my belly quivering, my pussy clamping down on him and squeezing him over and over again.

And then it was over, and we lay in a mess of arms and legs. Of sweat, and a few tears on my face.

I was a woman.

I was his.

And in this one brief moment in time, everything was perfect.

2 5

AXEL

I didn't want to move.

Balls deep in the sweetest, hottest woman I'd ever known, I wasn't going anywhere. I didn't want to speak or move or do anything to break the hot, sweaty spell that had us wrapped up.

Everything about that session had been perfect. Her body's reactions to me, her moans of pleasure. Even the way she touched me, kissed me, and the way she tasted. It was officially my sweetest memory of her. And the sexiest.

But as the seconds ticked on and Chastity was no longer panting, the room became still and quiet. Then I realized that despite my comfort and the fact that I didn't want to move, I was probably squashing her. "I should get up." I groaned, pushing up on my hands, my body complaining about the movement in every cell.

She grabbed for me, tightening her legs around my waist, and grabbing onto my arms. "No. Stay. You're not heavy."

I doubted that very much, but I didn't want to leave, either. So, I shifted a little and took some of my weight on my arm, then grabbed her hip and rolled to the side and dragged her with me. "Are you okay?"

She nodded, bliss etched into every crevice on her face. "Oh, yeah. How about you?"

"Yeah... I..." I shifted, and my dick slipped out of her. Damn. "I better clean up." I reached for my cock, searching for the lip of the condom that I always wore. Always. "What the..." I lifted her thigh to search for it, to stare down at her naked, perfect, pink little pussy. Wetness dripped out of her. "Oh my God."

"What's wrong?" Chastity asked, sitting up, then wincing. "Wow, that's kind of sore now."

Guilt hit me from every angle. I'd hurt her. I'd deflowered her. I'd had unprotected sex with a virgin. "Please tell me you're on the pill." Women did that, right? For other reasons other than sex.

"No. I don't need to. Why?" She glanced down at the same spot I'd been staring at. "Did you..."

I nodded and sat up, wanting to punch my own lights out. "I'm so sorry. I didn't even think. I just... you were..."

"I was what?" Chastity asked, her eyes wide and hurt.

I turned back and pulled her close. "No! You were perfect! So perfect! I just... let myself get carried away because you were so sexy." I kissed her forehead, then the tip of her nose. "Damn, you're beautiful. I could just lose myself in you all day."

She stared up at me with eyes that were still filled with tears. "I'm so sorry." She wiped her cheeks. "Should I be worried about anything?"

I shook my head. "Not from me. I get a full work up from the doctor every six months. Last blood test was a few weeks ago. Plus, I'm always careful."

She smiled, a tear slipping down her cheek making her look young and so vulnerable, she made my heart ache. "Not always."

I squeezed her tightly, hauling her closer. "You are a first for me, on so many levels, sweetheart. You're just..." I ran out of words. "Perfect."

She sighed and laid her head on my chest.

I rocked her, because it felt right to hold her like this. I glanced over at the clock on my dresser when I heard her softly yawn. "Hey, how 'bout we have a quick shower, then come back here to sleep?"

She slid off my lap then giggled as she swayed on her feet. "I can barely stand up properly. My legs are all wobbly."

I stood up behind her and slid a hand around her waist. "I'm sorry if I hurt you. I really didn't want to."

She smiled as we staggered into the bathroom. "You didn't hurt me, I'm just achy. I'm sure you know what that's like."

I chuckled. "Hardly. I can't say that my deflowering was very painful."

She rolled her eyes. "I don't want to know about that! What I meant was, I just used muscles I've literally never used before. You know, like when you train at the gym after a long break or something. I'm just achy."

"Okay, then." I agreed with her, she sounded drunk on her happiness. "Come and let's clean up." I turned on the shower, letting the water heat up for a few moments, and tugged her beneath the hot spray. I didn't know how to deal with all the different emotions coming at me. It was all too intense. How did people get any work done when they were in love like this?

I shook my head to get rid of the ridiculous thought. *Shut up! What is wrong with you?* I picked up the bar of soap and started washing her arms and pulled her close, so her back was against my chest. "As long as you're all right." I moved the soapy washcloth down between her legs, gently wiping away the remains of our first encounter.

"I'm more than all right." She sighed. "I'm great."

Waves of happiness flowed over me, and I began to feel like I might drown. I reached for the faucet handle to turn the water off. "Okay, let's get to bed."

"No! My turn." She reached for the soap and began washing my chest. "You're so sexy, I seriously can't believe it sometimes."

I took the soap from her and rinsed off. "Let's go, beautiful." Ushering her from the shower, I grabbed a couple of towels and dried us both quickly. "Let's get to bed." I put my arm around her and led her to my bed once again. "Jump in."

She crawled onto the mattress and lay down on her side, her profile as astounding as every other part of her. From the angle of her knee to the curve of her hip, she was just magnificent.

I crawled onto the mattress and tugged the blankets up over us, then laid my head on my pillow, facing her.

"You okay?" she asked.

I nodded. "Yeah, of course. Are you okay?"

She smiled softly. "I had the most amazing night ever. Of course, I'm all right. But you look worried. Are you regretting what happened?"

I grinned and grabbed for her. "Come here, you." I tugged her and flipped her over so that her spine was against my chest and her ass was pressed into my belly.

When she looked at me, it was like she was staring straight through me. "Are you sure you're okay, Axel? You can tell me."

I sighed and pressed a kiss to her shoulder. Even facing away, she was too in tune with me.

"I am a little worried. I've never risked unprotected sex like that. I..." If she got pregnant, what the hell would we do? Pat would kill me, and her college dreams would be done.

"It's okay. My period's due next week, so the timing isn't right, I don't think. But I'll let you know. Okay?"

"Okay."

What else could I say? It was my fault we were in this mess. It wasn't like the virgin should be the one to worry about contraception.

"Thank you for the most incredible night, Axel. I wouldn't change a thing, seriously. It was perfect."

I squeezed her tightly against me. "Let's get some sleep. I've been looking forward to this for a week."

She giggled softly. "Which part? Just sleeping with me?"

I closed my eyes. "Yeah. You're a good teddy bear."

It was so much more than that, but there was no way I was owning up to everything I was feeling at the moment. I felt too unguarded, too raw. Like someone had torn away all the armor I had carefully constructed around myself over the decades. Laying here with her sated body curled up in my arms, I was totally at peace. My brain wasn't whirling, I wasn't fighting. I was just me. Happy. And it was the most foreign feeling in the world.

"Go to sleep my, perfect girl. I've gotta get up early in the morning, but I'll wake you before I leave."

"Hmmmm." She nestled closer and was soon asleep.

I smiled and pulled the blanket a little higher over her shoulder, then slipped into dreamland alongside her.

WHEN I WOKE to my cell phone buzzing out my alarm. I groaned. I didn't want to get up. Today was going to be a bitch.

Chastity still slept in front of me, and I still had my arm wrapped around her. We'd barely moved all night.

I lifted my head and stared at the clock. Six a.m., and I didn't remember waking once. *Damn it, this girl is better for sleep than Valium.* I tried to remove my arm without waking her, but as soon as I tried to move away, she rolled onto her back, smiled up at me and blinked sleepily.

"Good morning."

"Good morning," I whispered back, dropping a quick kiss on her soft lips. "You stay asleep. I'll call you later."

She reached up and cupped my cheek softly. "Okay."

I dropped another kiss on her lips because the first one wasn't enough, then got out of the bed quickly before I was tempted to blow off my morning and stay in bed with her.

I raced to the shower, my cock hard and bouncing against my stomach. Damn it, I would have loved to take her again. Just roll on top and slide into her welcoming body. I was pretty sure she would have let me, if it hadn't been her first-time last night. I would have been rather late for work and driven us both into our first orgasm for the day.

And would you have remembered protection this time? Probably not, fucktard! "Damn it! What's wrong with you?"

If we were going to stay together longer-term, I would have asked her to go on the pill for us. Everything with her was so damn natural and easy. If we'd met a few hundred years ago, I'm sure I would have moved her in and had a dozen babies. There's no way I would have kept my hands to myself.

I grabbed my razor and quickly shaved. If I really felt that way about this girl, that in another time I would have happily pumped her full of babies, then what the hell was I doing letting her go in less than two weeks? I shook my head, cleaned up and headed into my walk-in closet. I picked out a custom navy pin-striped suit, a grey tie and my crispest white shirt.

It wasn't 1950. And we weren't Vikings or cavemen. I worked hard. She went to school. We were products of our society and our time, and I needed to be grateful for the moments I had with Chastity.

I glanced in the mirror to make sure I hadn't missed anything. Then I headed through my bedroom and out the door. I didn't look back, though a part of me ached to do so. I had a thousand things to do today, and I needed to get my mind focused, and off the young woman I'd left in my bed.

26

CHASTITY

I stared into the glass of white wine and ran my finger around the rim, softly singing to myself.

"Chastity? Are you okay?"

I glanced up. "Yeah, of course, Mom. Why?"

She shrugged and poured herself another glass of wine. "You just seem distracted that's all. Everything go well with Axel last night?"

I nodded, heat pumping into my cheeks, making my face burn. "Uh, yeah... great."

"Are you seeing him again?"

I stared at my mom, noting the pinched look around her mouth. "Yeah, I will. But don't worry, Mom, I know that there's no future for us. I'm just trying to enjoy it while it lasts." I brushed my hand past the wine glass I'd barely touched and reached for my cell phone. I'd been trying not to text Axel all day. After all, he hadn't reached out, but I'd looked at it so many times, it was embarrassing to admit the number.

"I just don't want you to get hurt, Chastity. You've always been so smart, avoiding boys like the plague. But this one..."

I laughed, "Hardly a boy, Mom."

"Exactly. He's a man. Who knows what he wants—or should."

I could feel my mother was ramping up for another one of her lectures, so I stood up, cell phone in hand. "I think I'm going to go to bed, Mom. See you in the morning?"

She nodded. "I've got to go into the office to pick something up, but then I'll be home in the afternoon."

"Perfect." I smiled. "I want to start baking Christmas cookies and some gingerbread." I kissed her on the cheek and headed to my bedroom. I needed a little space to think, and just be. My mom made it impossible to just be quiet. She always needed to fill the space with music, television or talk, even if it was idle chatter. And while I appreciated that most of the time, today I just needed some space.

I'd woken up around eleven a.m., having slept so well I could barely open my eyes from the sheer exhaustion of it all. But Axel was gone and had been for hours. The expensive penthouse apartment was enormous, cold, and empty without him. So, I'd thrown on my clothes, called an Uber, and raced out of there.

I didn't really like the idea of hanging around his space while he wasn't there. It would be just my luck that he'd have some maid or personal chef, or someone show up. And there I'd be, still wearing the dress I'd come over in last night. The walk of shame, billionaire style. If there was such a thing.

I'd gone home and spent the day with my mom, but now it was bedtime. I hadn't heard from him, and I missed him. I stripped out of my clothes, pulled back the blankets and climbed into bed in my panties and a tank top.

It was still early to go to bed—near ten—but I settled into my tiny mattress and sighed with happiness. Last night had been amazing. Better than any first-time sex story I'd ever heard. And it was all because Axel had been the most patient, perfect, talented lover. And I wanted more.

Hey. How was your day? I miss you.

I hit send, even though I wasn't sure if I should tell him how much I missed him. Would he like that? Hate it? Didn't matter now, it was gone into the ether.

Hey, stranger. I'm still at the office pulling an all-nighter. How was your day?

I frowned.

Seriously? I thought only slacker college students pulled all-nighters before final exams.

He wrote back.

Lol. Hardly.

I wriggled my fingers and tapped my foot against the bed. Should I ask to see him again? Would he want to see me soon? Or more like the weekend? I had no idea of his schedule, but if I had my way, I'd be in his bed again tomorrow. A cheeky thought popped into my head, and I smiled to myself and picked up my phone.

When you finally crash, do you want a teddy bear to sleep with?

I sent it then instantly regretted it. What if he said no? I jumped up and threw my phone on the bed when he didn't instantly respond. *Shit, shit, shit!*

Moving to the bathroom, I brushed my teeth, washed my face, and generally freaked out. I knew I wasn't one of those girls to over-think and over-stress about guys, but Axel was special. I didn't want to muck anything up before it had even begun. We'd agreed to spend time together over the next two weeks, and I wanted *all* those days.

When my nerves got the better of me, and my stomach twisted into knots, I raced back to my bedroom to find I'd missed a call from him. "Shit!" I paced my small bedroom while I rang him back. My heart was pounding and when he finally answered, my stomach lurched.

"Hey, beautiful."

The relief at hearing him talk to me in that tone was instant, and I staggered to my bed before collapsing onto the mattress. "I'm so sorry I missed your call. I was just in the bathroom."

"It's all good. I just thought it might be easier to chat for a minute. I need to get back to work soon."

"Oh." *Well, wasn't that romantic?*

"But I wanted to hear your voice once more. It'll bolster me for the hours ahead."

That's more like it! "Well, I was wondering if we could schedule our next date," I said in a rush. "We've only got two weeks before I head back and I want to see you as many times as I can, if that's okay." Damn, I was a mess.

He chuckled softly on the line. "How about tomorrow? I can't guarantee I'll be any use to you after the night's work I've got planned, but I'd love to see you."

I bit my lip to stop the squeal that rose from escaping. "I'd love that. What time?"

"How about eight?? My place again?"

"I'll be there."

"Great. I've gotta go, but I'll see you tomorrow."

The best words I'd ever heard. "Great. See you then." I hung up and let the squeal out. I was seeing him again! Tomorrow. *Your dad's best friend.* "Oh, shut up, "I told myself. Dad would never find out about our clandestine two weeks, surely. I would never tell him, and Axel certainly wouldn't either. So as long as neither of us went insane and said anything, he would always be none the wiser.

I put a hand to my still tender belly and smiled. Tomorrow would be amazing. More kisses, more sex, more intense, tender, ridiculously dream-like moments with Axel. I climbed into bed and ran my hands over my body, enjoying the tenderness of my nipples, and the sensitivity of my clit. Everything inside of me was buzzing with energy. And I wanted more of it. A lot more of it.

THE DAY DRAGGED on so slowly, I was going insane by the time seven p.m. rolled around.

"Are you sure you've had enough to eat?" Mom asked, offering me the Chicken Pad Thai for the tenth time.

"Yeah, I'm fine. I've gotta go pack, then I'll be off."

"You're going to Axel's again?"

I nodded, ignoring the unhappy look on my mom's face and her narrowed eyes. "Yep. Won't be long." I raced to my bedroom, packed a set of clothes for tomorrow and squirted some perfume on my neck. I'd been fantasizing all day about all the things I wanted to do to Axel. Maybe he'd teach me how to ride him? That had to be fun. Being able to look down on him, have him fondling my breasts while I slid up and down his cock. I shivered at the thought as I stuffed some clothes and a toothbrush into my bag.

Mom opened the door as I was pulling out my cell phone. "I'll drive you."

"No, it's okay," I said, waving my phone. "I was just about to—"

"No!" She interrupted, crossing her arms over her chest. "I want to see where you're heading off to every night." From the look on her face and the set of her jaw, this wasn't an argument I was going to win.

"Okay, Mom. That'd be great." Hopefully she wouldn't insist on seeing his actual apartment, though if she did, would she change her mind about him? Money and success generally impressed her, though, it hadn't so far with Axel. But maybe she didn't realize just how rich he actually was. "You ready to go right away?" I asked, glancing at my watch. "I said I'd be there at eight."

Mom nodded and stepped out of my doorway. "Yep, let's go."

We locked up and jumped into her old car.

"You'll need to direct me. I don't know which way I'm going."

"Just head to the city, and I'll show you," I said, pointing down the street. "It's about twenty minutes or so."

Mom nodded, and we took off.

The silence was deafening, so I reached for the radio and flicked on the knob.

"Where does he live?" she asked suddenly. "An apartment?"

"Yeah. The penthouse, in a building in the city," I answered, feeling strangely un-nerved by my mother's behavior. She seemed angry, though I couldn't work out why she would be.

"The penthouse?" she repeated. "Impressive, I suppose."

I laughed then coughed to clear my throat. "No, what's impressive is the fact he built and owns the whole building."

Silence descended again, so this time I just looked out the window and watched the city fly by.

As we got closer, I started directing her along the streets, until finally she pulled up outside the impressive building. "Thanks, Mom. Did you want to walk me up? Or—"

She shook her head emphatically, effectively interrupting me, and I turned away to open the door.

Her hand snaked out and she grabbed my arm. "Please be careful, Chastity."

I turned back. "What do you mean, Mom? What's wrong?"

"I just..." She stopped and swallowed. "You know I've never regretted keeping you."

"I know."

"But you have an opportunity here that I never had. You're smart. You're amazing. You're heading to graduation, and chiropractic school, and I don't want you throwing any of that away on some guy. I don't care how rich he is."

I smiled and squeezed her hand. "I won't, Mom. Axel is just... fun. He makes me feel special."

"I know, that's what I'm afraid of," she said, then withdrew her hand. "He isn't the marrying kind, sweetheart. So just guard your heart as best you can, okay? You're not the type of girl who has fun and just walks away."

I rolled my eyes and got out of the car. "Thanks for the lift, Mom! I'll see you tomorrow."

I stepped back and waved at her as she pulled into traffic and drove home.

I wrapped my arms around myself and thought about what she'd said. In the past I hadn't been one to date guys casually, and I didn't really think I was now either. But I wanted some fun, and I deserved it after all the time and effort I'd put in to being "good" during my teenage years. It was time to be bad.

27

AXEL

My head throbbed with a migraine, and I was beginning to see stars. The aura had been chasing me all day. Then the light sensitivity had hit, and I had my driver take me home, and I'd climbed into bed. When the doorbell peeled, I groaned. Loudly. "Oh, shit."

I didn't keep a permanent housekeeper like most of my wealthy friends, but at times like this, I wished I did. I rolled out of bed, only opening my eyes enough to see where I was going and felt my way along the walls to the front door. When I opened it and saw my gorgeous little Chastity there, even in my pained state, a sense of happiness washed over me.

Her face was lit up with a huge smile that quickly crashed into a frowning look of worry. "What's wrong? Are you okay?"

I waved her inside then shut the door after her, sagging against the wall for a moment to stop from falling over. "Migraine."

"Then you should be in bed," she said, dropping her bag on the ground, then putting her body next to mine and my arm over her shoulder. "Come on. I'll help you."

I didn't fight her as she walked me back to my room, supporting my wobbly frame.

When I got close to my bed, I pulled my arm off her shoulders, staggered over to the mattress, and climbed beneath the covers again. The room was dark and cool, and I sighed as my head hit the pillow once more. "I'm sorry to screw up our night," I managed to say, though I could barely open my eyes.

She laughed softly. "You're just trying to get out of having sex with me again, aren't you?"

I chuckled as well. "I wish that was the reason." I stifled the groan that rose as a fresh wave of nausea rolled through me.

"What do you need?" she asked quietly. "Water? Painkillers?"

"Just sleep," I told her. I'd already taken everything I had. This was most likely stress induced. I'd had a bitch of a day.

The mattress dipped as Chastity crawled onto the bed, lay down beside me and pulled the covers up over us.

I forced my eyes open to stare at her. "Are you tired too?"

She smiled as she laid her head on the pillow and reached out to run her fingers through my hair.

I moaned at the touch. "God, that feels good."

She pressed harder, massaging my temples in a rhythmic circular motion.

"If you roll onto your back and turn this way a little, I can do both sides at the same time."

"Okay." That sounded like heaven, though I'd never thought that was a place I'd end up. I rolled onto my back and moved so that I was lying at more of a horizontal angle.

Chastity sat up, shuffled into place at the headboard, and gently put my head in her lap.

"I'm sorry," I said again, at a total loss for words with so much pain winging through my usually healthy body. "I don't usually get migraines this bad, but..."

"But what?" she whispered. "Are you okay?"

I nodded while she rubbed her fingers over my temples, then began to slowly trace patterns over my skull and through my hair. "Yeah, I'm okay. Just work shit. That feels really nice." The pain was actually easing a little. Not enough to stand up or try to function, but I might be able to fall asleep if the pressure decreased a little.

"My chiropractor does a lot of cranial work on me, and I know it might help a little."

I sighed again as she worked through my skull, all the way around the back where my neck ached with tension. "Pity you're not trained yet," I joked. "I'd hire you full time to look after me and my staff."

"How many people work for you?" she asked.

"Hmmm... in my building? I don't know. Two hundred, maybe."

She laughed softly. "Two hundred people, check them twice a month, a hundred people a week. Yeah. That sounds like a good plan."

I smiled and relaxed deeper into her touch. I'd said it as a joke, but I knew of CEOs that hired massage therapists to attend their staff. Why not a full-time chiropractor?

"Let's set it up," I said. "You call me when you graduate, and we'll get you an office."

She was silent for a long time until I opened my eyes and looked up at her. "You okay?"

She nodded. "Yeah, that sounds nice. Close your eyes. Try to sleep."

She sounded sad, and I got it. We'd set the terms of this deal already. Two weeks of sex and fun, then we were done. Now I was inviting her to come work for me. That hadn't been part of the plan.

"I didn't mean to—"

"It's okay," she interrupted quietly. "I'm enjoying the time we're having now and not thinking about the future."

I smiled and closed my eyes. "You can't be enjoying this."

"I am," she jumped in to say. "I don't mean the part about you being in pain, that's shit. And I must admit that I'd planned to already be naked with you like this. But my plans included me massaging other parts of your body."

I groaned. "Oh, God... don't torture me. I wish I could. God, I wish I could."

But my cock didn't even stir at the suggestion, which, considering how much I desired the woman in my bed, definitely said something about my current state. All of my blood was pumping into my migraine, and my body was not responding to anything other than the pain.

She giggled. "I'm sorry, I said that all around the wrong way. What I meant was... I'm kind of enjoying looking after you. I didn't think you'd let me."

I couldn't help the sigh that fell from my lips. "Yeah... well..."

"I mean, you don't have full-time staff members cooking and cleaning for you. I doubt you let a lot of people cater to you. You just don't seem like that sort of guy."

I sighed again and didn't open my eyes. I felt vulnerable enough as it was. "How come you seem to know me so well?" I'd never let anyone see me like this before. Not since I was sixteen and living with my parents. Though even then, it was the housekeeper that brought me a barf bucket, not my mother.

It took a lot for me to trust anyone, let alone a woman I was sleeping with. That didn't happen often, and to let them see me in this sort of state... useless, helpless, and vulnerable? She was right. It had never happened. "Come lie down with me." I said, tugging at her arms. "I wanna feel that naked body of yours against me."

"Okay, give me a minute. Just gotta run to the bathroom."

She crawled off the bed and disappeared.

So I took my time shuffling around and lying my head back on the pillow. The pain had eased, and the nausea was only softly clawing at my stomach. I might be able to sleep for a few hours, then I'd feel better. I was sure of it.

The door closed and Chastity crawled back into the bed with me.

"You better be naked," I softly growled at her.

She giggled and shuffled closer, shoving her naked, fleshy, warm ass against my belly.

"Oh, yeah," I said, wrapping my arm around her middle.

"You're not naked though," she whispered.

I pulled her even closer, then kissed her hair. "I couldn't stand up long enough to undress properly. Don't worry. As soon as I can get naked. I will."

She didn't say anything else, she just settled into my arms and was still. And quiet.

Sleep beckoned and yet I fought it, not wanting to lose touch of this moment.

We'd had so many perfect, beautiful times together. And this one, amazingly, was going to be tattooed across my mind for many years to come. The poor girl had come here looking for fun, passion, and orgasms. And here I was, still dressed, cuddling her in bed, totally unable to fulfil any of the fantasies she'd hoped for.

"Thank you for this," I whispered at her before I lost my mind and succumbed to sleep. "I'll make it up to you, I promise." I didn't hear what she said next, if she did respond. Sleep claimed my drug-addled, pained body, and into dream world I fell.

28

CHASTITY

I was in love with Axel. There was no denying it any longer. And due to this fact, I'd concluded that I was an idiot. An absolute imbecile.

I was lying in his bed, horny, hot, and naked, and wiggling against his sleeping body. Well, no, I was lying as still and quiet as I could, because I knew he was asleep. His breathing had changed, and his arms were heavy around me.

But the fact that he was asleep didn't stop me from knowing just how much I wanted him. How much I loved the fact that he'd wanted me close to him while he was sick. He was not the sort of man to let people in unless he trusted them.

And here I was, being held by him, while he slept off a migraine. I felt honored. And dumb at the same time. Dumb because I'd known this guy was trouble from the moment I'd laid eyes on him. From the very second I'd seen him walk through those doors at Dad's gym, I'd known this was the sort of guy who broke the hearts of girls like me. But how was I going to walk away from this with my head, and preferably my heart, still in one piece?

Inside my mind, in that place I didn't want to admit really existed, that part of my brain was already working out how far school was from here, and whether I could get a ride home on weekends to see him. But would he want that? He'd said that we only had two weeks together, but would he want more if I offered it to him?

This cuddle and trust told me he'd jump at the chance to keep his teddy bear. That he'd keep seeing me as long as it worked for the both of us. But then there was the whole Dad thing, the complicating factor. The longer we were together, the more likely it was that my father would find out, and neither of us wanted that.

And there was one other shitty thing to deal with. The fact that I was in love with the guy and wanted to stay with him forever despite my future plans, our deal, and the knowledge inside my brain that said this was not the man to fall for. This was the kind of guy you had fun with. *And I was.* I was having lots of fun.

But as I closed my eyes and willed my body not to clench in anticipation of what he would do next, I wanted to admit to myself finally that he was so much more. He was passionate, and kind, and extremely hardworking. He was a man to admire, to love, to marry. I shook my head and growled at myself.

Stop it! You've got, like, ten days left. Enjoy it, because soon enough you'll be taking the tattered remains of your heart back to college, and the only thing you'll have to hold at night will be the memories of nights like this.

29

AXEL

aking up without throbbing pain in my head was like sunshine after the storm. My head was clear, but my body ached with an intense hangover-like feeling. I opened my eyes and stared down at Chastity, where she lay sleeping in my arms. Damn, she'd been amazing last night. Compassionate, patient. Behaving so far beyond her years, which she often did.

"Good morning," she said suddenly, her eyes still closed. "Are you feeling better?" She rolled onto her back and the blankets slipped down, revealing her gorgeous breasts and rosy, pink nipples. She opened her eyes and smiled.

A wave of lust washed over me. "Hmmm... much better." I said, tugging the blankets further down to reveal her full nakedness and the surprise she'd obviously wanted to reveal last night. "Did you shave for me?" I asked, admiring her newly bare flesh as I ran my hand up her thigh and over the freshly manicured strip of hair covering her mons.

She giggled and opened her legs, inviting me to touch her. "You never said anything, but I thought you might like it a little neater. Oh..."

I used my fingertips to circle her clit, then dipped down to where she was already juicy for me. "You feel ready, sweetheart. Have you been thinking about what I should have done to you last night?" Because I certainly was. I couldn't believe a stupid migraine had cost me a whole night with this beautiful woman. And I intended to make up for it now.

I flicked her clit from side to side with my fingers, then bent my head to kiss her mouth. I tasted her tongue with mine as I slid a single finger down between her lips and inside her wet, tight channel.

She groaned against my mouth, then pulled me down on top of her.

I thrust my finger in and out of her sweet, hot opening, loving the way her pussy tightened and clenched around me.

She threw her head back, moaning loudly, which made her breasts arch invitingly into the air.

I moved down and clamped my lips around one tight, plump little nipple and suckled gently.

She threaded her fingers through my hair and held me to her.

My cock was pulsing now, throbbing and hard. But I ignored it, determined to give her the pleasure she craved.

Suddenly she pushed on my chest, and I went with her motions, rolling onto my back. "What are you doing?"

"I want to get on top of you," she insisted, reaching for my sweats and tugging them down over my hips.

I laughed at her display of impatience.

She tugged at my pants, so I lifted my hips and let her undress me. She slid everything down my legs, then threw them to the floor.

When she crawled up to me, I wanted nothing more than to grab her around the waist and haul her on top of me, but I stopped myself. "Grab a condom from the top drawer."

Her eyes went wide with surprise then she grinned and crawled over to the nightstand where I had a new stash.

I went up on my elbows and stared after her, loving the view her round ass afforded me as she rifled through my drawer. She was sexy and lush, and I couldn't wait to lick her from head to toe.

When she crawled back, she had a "cat that ate the canary" smile as she handed me the rubber and I ripped it open. But before I could slide it on, she was on her belly, grabbing me and wrapping her lips around my cock.

"Fuck!" I cried out, grabbing hold of the sheets beneath me. "Damn, your mouth is perfect."

She moved her hand up and down the shaft while she sucked on the head, tonguing the lip like I'd taught her.

"Come here," I demanded, tugging at her arm until she lifted her head and looked at me.

"What's wrong?"

Nothing! "Come ride me."

I rolled the condom down over my pulsing cock and pulled her up until she was straddling me and rubbing her wet pussy over my belly.

"How do I do this exactly?" she asked.

I groaned at how sweet and innocent yet totally hot she was. I grabbed the shaft and held it up at an angle. "Go up on your knees, tilt your pelvis back, and slide down."

She frowned, the most adorable look of concentration on her face as she moved back and wiggled around, coating my cock with her juices and driving me crazy.

My head fell back on a moan when she finally found the entrance to her body and slid back, wrapping me in tight heat.

"Oh... wow," she moaned as she inched back.

I grabbed her tiny waist and squeezed her, trying to hold onto the slim piece of sanity I still possessed.

"Now I move?" she panted out.

I nodded, opening my eyes even though I hadn't realized I'd closed them, and staring up at her. "Yeah. You move."

She began to roll her hips, and lift up and slide down, slowly driving me crazy with her wet heat.

I groaned and threw my head back, loving the sensations ricocheting through my body while the gorgeous woman on top of me gasped out her own pleasure.

Everything about her was addictive, and I liked her innocence a little bit more than I should have. I loved the fact she was learning with me. That I was her first *everything*. I lifted my head again and forced my drugged eyes to open so that I didn't miss the expression on her face as she learned how much she liked being on top of me. What I saw tugged at my heart. Her eyes were wide, her mouth open in wonder. She leaned down to kiss me, and I reached up, cupping her face, and arching up to meet her lips.

We kissed deeply, weaving our tongues together and meshing our mouths, just as our bodies were entwining. She kept moving on top of me, taking my cock deep into her body, then withdrawing until I couldn't stand the slow pace anymore.

I planted my feet on the mattress and gripped her hips, driving up into her with every downward thrust she made.

"Oh! Axel!" Chastity grabbed onto my wrists, anchoring herself.

"Do you want... me... to... stop?" I asked with every heavy thrust into her tightening pussy.

She closed her eyes and shook her head. "No. Don't stop. Please." She was flushed with heat, her cheeks pink and her chest heaving as she gasped and moaned.

I drove into her harder, faster, fighting back the edges of my own orgasm. Heat tingled at the base of my spine and trickled down the back of my legs, but I fought it off, determined to have Chastity find her pleasure before I did.

"Axel, don't stop. Please, don't stop. Oh, fuckkkk." Chastity bucked against me, coming so hard it felt like she was going to squeeze my dick off. She shuddered over me, her nails digging into my hands.

I had no choice now. I thrust up into her, as hard and high as I could, damning the stupid rubber between us. I roared so loud I probably peeled the paint off the walls. I saw stars. And when I finally fell from the heavens, I had an angel on top of me, cuddling into my chest and sighing with contentment.

30

CHASTITY

It was Christmas Eve morning, and the day could not have started off any better. My body was still tingling from Axel's magical touch, and as I lay here on top of his chest, I didn't want to go anywhere. "What are your plans for today?" I asked, twisting my fingers in his chest hair.

"Um..." He wrapped his arms around my back and kissed the top of my head. "I probably need to finish all that work I didn't manage to get done last night. How about you?"

I smiled against him, wishing I had the guts to lick his skin and taste just how sweet his sweat was. "I'll be baking with my mom, mostly. Wrapping presents. All that stuff." I might catch up with Nicola later too. I hadn't seen my best friend in far too long.

"And tomorrow? You'll be visiting with your parents?" he asked, his throat catching as he said the words.

I turned around and brought my hand up, resting my chin on my fingers that lay on his chest. He looked so adorable. A little red in the cheeks, drowsy-eyed. "You look like you want to go back to sleep."

He chuckled, his chest moving up and down beneath me. "Yeah, well, you'll wear me out at this rate."

I laughed this time too, finally rolling off him and stretching out the slight ache in my legs. "I doubt that very much."

"Can I interest you in a shower?" he asked, running his hand over my ribcage and cupping my breast.

I looked at him with a fake irritation. "Haven't you had enough?"

He mock frowned at me. "Of you? Never! Want me to prove it?"

My breath hitched with excitement at the request. Could I handle more sex this morning? I was feeling pretty good. "Where? In the shower?"

He rolled off the bed, dropped the condom in the wastebasket and beckoned to me. "Yeah. Why? Do you want to be taken in the shower? Have you been thinking about it?"

I got to my feet, swallowing my nerves down. "Yeah, there's something so sexy about being taken against a wall."

Axel reached out and took my hand, pulling me towards him so hard I stumbled into his chest. "I find it so sexy that you have these fantasies about us. Wanna share anymore?"

Heated embarrassment rushed into my face. "Um... Do I have to tell you them all now?"

He chuckled. "Of course not. But once I fulfil this fantasy for you, you've gotta give me another one."

I shivered all over with the promise in his voice. "Okay."

He grinned and dropped a kiss on my lips that made me quiver all over again. "Well, let's get to that shower scene then."

He tugged me into the shower and beneath the hot water, then proceeded to show me that despite being nearly twice my age, his sexual appetite was in no way lacking. In fact, I doubted anyone my age would be able to compete with him. And that made me feel more grateful than anything else.

I had a god of a man. *A sex god.* And he was all mine. For one more week.

∾

I WOKE up Christmas morning with bleary eyes and a soft tension sort of headache that came from being dehydrated. And still tired. I rolled onto my back and stretched my arms above my head, enjoying the loud groan that echoed through the room as I relaxed once again into the warmth of my bed. Christmas day had always been my favorite holiday. Too much food and chocolate. Sleeping late, no study, and time with my parents.

Mom and Dad, being only twenty-one years older than me, had always been fun parents. They had lots of energy and cool friends, and Christmas had always been magical. But as I reached for my cell phone and saw a thoughtful message from Axel, my chest squeezed with pain.

Missing him today would keep me preoccupied. I really was falling head over heels for the guy, and I knew that my most anticipated day of the year was going to be lackluster without him. It was wrong of me to assume that I wouldn't have a good day, but the feeling was there, and it was going to take a lot of effort to shake that mood.

"Good morning!" Mom called, opening the door, carrying in a mug of hot chocolate and the first of my presents. This was a tradition at our house. A present for breakfast, a present before lunch, and a final present before I went to my father's place for dinner.

"Merry Christmas, Mom," I responded, smiling as I dragged myself up to sit in bed. "Thank you."

I took the hot chocolate from her and couldn't help but smile as she handed me a gift, a box the size of a new pair of shoes, wrapped in red paper with a green ribbon. Maybe today wouldn't be too bad after all. I took a sip of my hot chocolate, then the doorbell rang.

Mom's eyes brows furrowed. "Who on earth could that be?"

Shrugging, I set the mug down and began to pull at the ribbon around the box.

Mom got up and tightened the tie around her fluffy housecoat. "I'll go see who that is and grab you some of the gingerbread we made yesterday."

"Perfect breakfast. Thanks, Mom." And it really was. I loved gingerbread so much, especially when it was a little soft and perfect for dunking in hot drinks.

When my mother got back to my room, she had a worried furrow going on between her eyes.

"What's up?" I asked, finally tearing open the paper to reveal exactly what I expected. "Oh, wonderful. Thank you so much, Mom." A new pair of flat leather boots. "These will be perfect for next year."

Mom held in her hands a small box, wrapped in familiar post office paper. "This was delivered for you."

I almost laughed, but that didn't seem appropriate. "On Christmas day? Who delivers Christmas day?"

Mom handed me the box and sat down on my bed once more. "It was a special courier. In a suit."

My heart leapt. *Surely, it couldn't be.* I tore open the paper to reveal a small, black jewelry box with a tiny gift tag attached.

"Were you expecting a gift from Axel?" Mom asked, the words falling into the silence around us.

My heart thudded in my chest. "No, not at all." I flipped over the gift tag, and it read, "To Chastity. Merry Christmas. Love, Axel." My eyes burned with unexpected tears, and I held the box in my hand for a long minute. I didn't want to open it up and break the spell. I wanted to believe just for a moment that he cared for me the way I cared for him.

"Open it, Chastity. The suspense is killing me."

I burst into laughter and wiped away the stray tear that fell. "Okay. Okay." I popped open the lid and gasped. Inside was the most beautiful necklace. There was a thin silver or white gold chain. And hanging at the end of the chain was a floating single diamond the size of a pea. "Uh..."

"That can't be real," Mom said from beside me. She'd moved to stand behind me and was peering over my shoulder.

"I don't know if it is, or if it isn't." I was breathless, taking the necklace out of its velvet bed and holding it up into the air. "Would you put it on me?" The tears were gathering in my eyes once more and my nose was tingling.

Mom clipped the necklace around the back of my neck, and I stood up and rushed over to the mirror.

"It's beautiful," I whispered, loving the way the jewel shimmered and shone in the morning light.

"If that's real, Chastity, do you have any idea how much it would have cost?"

I shook my head. "No. And I don't care." I twisted around and pulled my robe from the back of my chair. "Should we stay in our pajamas all morning before we go to Grandma's? Or do you want to do showers first?"

My mom crossed her arms over her chest, looking thoroughly displeased. "You can't wear that all day, Chastity. It'll raise too many questions."

I forced a smile to my lips, trying to shrug off my mother's mood. "It's freezing today, Mom. I'll wear a sweater, and no one will even see it."

Mom continued to pout at me, so I opened my door. "Let's go get some cookies and start our day right. I have your first present under the tree too, if you'd like to open it?"

That made her smile, but the rest of the day with her was just the same. Stilted. Odd. I didn't want to ask her why she was being so strange, because I knew she'd say something horrible about Axel, then I'd get upset and everything would get thrown out of balance even more.

It was a relief when it was finally five p.m., and I could head over to my dad's house for dinner.

"I love you, Mom. See you tomorrow."

"You're sleeping at your dad's tonight?" she asked, frowning.

"Ah, yeah. I always do Christmas night." That had been the arrangement for longer than I could remember. Mom had always had Christmas Eve, and most of Christmas day.

Dad had gotten dinner and the night of Christmas.

"But I feel like I've barely seen you this week." Mom pouted again.

"You've been staying at your dad's and Axel's, and I expected to spend a lot more time with you than I have."

I hugged her tightly. "I love you. I'll see you tomorrow, okay?" When I pulled back, Mom simply nodded, and I grabbed my gifts for Dad and headed off to the Uber waiting outside.

There was a thread of anger I couldn't ignore pulsing through my gut. How dare my mother be so selfish? I'd spent more time with her than *anyone* else. But as she'd pointed out, she was used to unfettered, unlimited time with me. Maybe I'd spoiled her? But I didn't think it was unreasonable to ask for a little time with the guy I was seeing. I was twenty-one already. I should have been dating like this for years.

The Uber drove me to my father's apartment, and I got out of the car juggling my backpack and the presents I'd brought with me. I was still annoyed with my mom. She'd done nothing but pout all day. From the moment I'd received that present from Axel, she'd been uninterested in me.

The gifts I'd given her were greeted with a simple smile, and she'd been silent for most of lunch. I didn't know what her problem was, but if Axel's presence in my life was the issue, I didn't want to fix her problem. I went up to Dad's apartment and was greeted by the sounds of my aunts and uncles and cousins.

"Chastity!" I was pulled into the vortex of hugs, food, and presents.

By the time they all left, I was exhausted, and had collapsed on the armchair, looking at my dad with a silly grin on my face. "That was a fun night. Thank you."

He gestured to the bowls of candies and chocolates that still decorated the coffee table. "Do you want anything else?"

I shook my head and grabbed for my full belly. "God, no. I'm stuffed." I sighed and leaned my head back. I had a headache again. It was so tiring to pretend that everything was okay, when it wasn't.

"Hey, Chastity?"

"Yeah, Dad?" I lifted my head to see his concerned look.

"Are you all right? I mean... you haven't seemed yourself tonight."

"Oh, just had a bit of a fight with Mom," I said, blaming the easiest option, which was mostly true. "I'm sorry if that affected our night. I didn't mean for it to."

"Oh, no," he said, waving his hand to dismiss me. "You've been great. I just can tell that you aren't your normal self."

I missed Axel so much it hurt. That was the main reason for my mood, but I couldn't admit that to my father. "Thanks again for my gift, Dad. The bag for school is just perfect." He had bought me an expensive, black leather satchel that I loved. It would be able to hold my laptop, books, and anything else I needed.

"Glad you liked it," Dad said, then hauled himself to his feet. "I think I'm going to hit the hay. How about you?"

I got to my feet with an exaggerated groan. "I might take a hot shower first, if that's okay."

He came forward and pressed a kiss to my forehead. "Of course, sweetheart."

I hugged him tightly, just for a moment. "Merry Christmas, Daddy."

He held me for another minute, then we drifted apart. "Night!"

I went to my bedroom and pulled out my cell phone. I'd made myself hide it through the day, so I wasn't distracted or focused on Axel. It hadn't worked. I'd ached for my lifeline to him. He'd message again.

Call me when you have a minute.

It was almost eleven p.m. but I called him, anyway, sinking down onto the bed when I heard his voice.

"Hey, sexy. Merry Christmas."

"Merry Christmas," I managed to say back, using my sleeve to wipe my running nose. "Thank you so much for the necklace you sent to my house. It's totally incredible."

Axel's chuckle made my heart squeeze in my chest. "I saw it and thought of you. I had to buy it."

"Well, you shouldn't have."

He laughed again. "Why not?"

"I don't deserve it," I whispered, on the verge of tears now, which annoyed the hell out of me. I'd done such a good job of holding them in all day.

"Are you okay, sweetheart?"

I nodded and swallowed the sob that rose. Damn it. I missed him so much, it hurt.

31

AXEL

I'd been working all day, forcing myself into the CEO frame of mind, Concentrating on the merger, business, financials and growth of my company. Important things for my life, my future. Things that would normally have me focused and enthusiastic. Instead, I was finding it almost impossible to focus. Why? Because I missed her.

I wasn't a romantic, nor a sap. Christmas day hadn't meant much to me since I was a kid. And even then, my parents hadn't exactly made it a warm and fuzzy time for me, like all the other kids I knew. But today I'd ached for the type of Christmas I knew that Chastity was having. Without me. Surrounded by family, presents, food, and cuddles. I felt as lonely as the first snowflake of the season. And as desperate for company.

"Do you want to come over?" I asked, the words leaving my mouth before I thought them over properly.

There was silence on the end of the line. "Ah... I'd love to. But I can't." Her regret seemed genuine, but it was still a stab in the gut. She couldn't be with me—or didn't want to.

"Oh, yeah, I understand," I rushed in to say, standing up from my desk and stretching my legs by walking around my apartment, nervous energy pulsing through my veins. "It's Christmas. I get it. You have to stay with your family."

Another heavy silence filled the other end of the phone.

"I wish I could..."

"Don't worry about it." I said, crossing my arms over my chest. "I get it. I'm not family. It's Christmas. No worries." Now I sounded like a petulant child. I rolled my eyes heavenward and bit the inside of my cheek. *Fuck. Now I'd scared her off.* "Chastity, I..."

"Please don't say any more," she whispered, then a sob echoed into my ears, and my heart broke.

"I'm sorry," I groaned out, clenching my free hand into a fist, and glancing towards the nearest wall. Damn, I'd like to put my fist right into that. "It's just that I miss you too. And I want to see you."

"I want to see you too!" she burst out. "Do you know how hard it's been for me today? To pretend that I was happy to be with my family when all I wanted to do was run over to your place and curl up in your lap? Christmas is my favorite day of the year, Axel. My favorite day. The tree, the presents, the food. My family."

"You had all of that," I bit out. "Then what was the problem?"

"I wasn't with you!" she practically screamed through the phone. "It wasn't supposed to be like this. We were meant to have a casual, no-strings-attached few weeks and I..." She stopped and I heard her gulp.

My heart began to pick up pace, pounding a little harder, and a little louder against my ribcage. "You what?"

"I already told you," She repeated, sighing heavily. "I spent the whole day wishing I was at your place, curled up in your lap rather than where I was, spending Christmas with my family."

She sighed again, and I went and sat down on the sofa, my excess energy now gone.

"It wasn't supposed to be like this," she said again. "I ache when I'm not with you."

"Fuck." I groaned and slid onto my back on the couch. "I want you with me too. Always. Even when I should be working, I want you."

The silence fell between us again, but this time, I could almost hear her smiling down the line.

"So... can I come over tomorrow morning? After breakfast, maybe?"

I grinned. "Definitely. Anything particular you want to do?"

"I want to thank you for my present."

There was so much promise in her voice, my hormones surged in response.

"Are you wearing it?" I asked her. "Or did your mother confiscate it the moment she saw it?" It would be just like that woman.

Chastity giggled on the end of the line. "She tried. But I put it on and hid it beneath my sweater and wore it all day. I'm never going to take it off."

I closed my eyes. Fuck it, I was in too deep here. And I wasn't treading water anymore, I was drowning. *Happily* drowning.

If any other girl of my past had waxed lyrical about how much she missed me, and how attached she'd grown to a gift, I would have cut her off without a second thought. Clingy, emotional females were not my *schtick*. But with Chastity... damn it I wanted to drive to her father's place, pick her up, and bring her home to my bed. *Exactly where she's meant to be.*

I shook myself and sat up. "Do you want me to pick you up in the morning?"

"No, I'll get to your place."

A calmness settled over me as my stomach flipped. "What time?"

She laughed, breaking the tension that had fallen over the phone call. "Are you that desperate to see me?"

My breath whistled through my teeth as I inhaled sharply. "I wouldn't say desperate."

"Okay. How's two p.m.?"

"Uh..." *No!*

"One p.m.?"

This time I heard the amusement in her voice, and I couldn't stop the answering smile that pulled at my lips. "Just get your ass over here as soon as possible, okay?"

She laughed her sweet, luscious ass off at that one. "I will. Good night."

"Sweet dreams," I said, then hung up.

I set my phone down and swung my legs around again to lie back on the couch, staring up at the ceiling. What had that girl done to me? I'd been fighting a strange sort of weariness all day. I didn't want to call it depression, but damn I'd been in a shitty mood. Now? I wanted to laugh and jump around. *Fucking hell*, I was in so much trouble with this girl.

I'd never felt this way before, and I had no idea what to even *do* with all the feelings. I rolled off the couch and went to find my running gear, needing to work through this restlessness somehow. Then, tomorrow, I'd fuck us both into sweet, sweet oblivion.

32

CHASTITY

I tried not to rush through breakfast with my father at a gorgeous little café on the corner, but I was bouncing up and down to go. I inhaled my eggs benedict and hugged him tightly. "Thank you so much for breakfast, and last night, Dad. It was all great." I grabbed up all my things, including my new bag, and my father's hand snaked out to grab my arm.

"Hey, sweetheart."

"Yeah?"

"Are you seeing someone?"

My gut tightened like I'd taken a punch. "What do you mean?"

He threw down some cash on the check and stood up with a grin. "You've been distracted, jumpy, and I know you're rushing off to see someone. Who is it?"

I inhaled sharply and pressed a hand to my stomach. "It's really new. I haven't told anyone."

Dad grinned even brighter. "I knew it! Good for you. I've been worried about you at times—all work and no fun. I hope your mom and my choices haven't put you off chasing love, Chastity, because that would make me feel terrible."

I relaxed and smiled at my handsome father. "I've waited for several reasons, and I don't regret a single minute of it. Because now I've found someone I think is really special, and I..." I stopped and shrugged, not sure what else I could say without giving the game away.

"As long as he thinks you're special too. Wait... it's a *he*, right?"

I laughed. "Yes, Dad."

"Not that there's anything wrong with you wanting whoever you want. As long as they take care of you."

My poor father was blushing now, and I rushed him for another hug. "It's all good, Dad. I'll see you on the weekend, yeah?"

He nodded. "Do you want me to drop you off?"

"No. It's not far. Love you."

"Love you too."

I waved as I walked down the street and around the corner. Axel's place was only a few blocks away, but I wasn't walking that far carrying my new bag and all my stuff from last night. I arranged an Uber, which arrived in a few short minutes. Then I was speeding towards Axel's apartment, my heart in my throat. I couldn't believe how excited and happy I was.

When the driver dropped me off, I raced up to the elevator and hopped from foot to foot as I sped up to the penthouse.

When the doors opened, Axel wasn't waiting for me in the living room, he was pacing the foyer, a few feet from the elevator's entrance. "Hey!" His face lit up with a smile I felt like I'd waited my whole life to see.

I dropped my bags to the ground with a clatter and ran for him like I was in a blockbuster rom-com and my life depended on it.

He opened his arms as I jumped at his chest, pressing myself into his powerful body and wrapping my arms around his neck. His lips came down on mine, hot and possessive, and I clung to him, never wanting the kiss to end. And it didn't, for so long.

Axel's hands came up to cup my face, and he slowed his kiss, taking his time to nibble at my lips and taste me. By the time he finally raised his head, I couldn't open my eyes and swayed so badly I knocked into him. "Whoa, there," he said as he tugged me against him.

I grinned up at him, opening my eyes enough to see him through half lids. "What did you do to me? I feel totally drugged."

He chuckled and hugged me again, holding me so close I could feel his heart beating against my chest. "Let's go relax on the couch for a bit."

I didn't want to argue, though I would have preferred he dragged me to bed with him. "Okay." I collapsed onto the couch when we finally reached it, and Axel tugged me into his lap. I turned around so I could face him, half lying across him, and burrowed into his arms. I breathed in his scent that was so uniquely Axel and sighed. "God, this feels good."

He didn't respond, but his answering sigh said it all.

We'd both fallen into this relationship with the best of intentions of parting in a few days, but I already knew that on my end at least, that was going to be one hell of a day.

"Chastity... I..." Axel's phone suddenly went off in his pocket and he groaned. "I'm so sorry, let me just turn that off." He lifted up, pulled out his phone, then stared at the screen. He went deathly still.

"What's wrong?" I asked.

His gaze shifted to me. "It's your dad."

My heart leapt in my throat. "Don't answer it."

"But what if he's planning on coming over here?" he asked. "Pat turned up the other day for a run and didn't even call first."

I swallowed hard, then nodded once. *Fuck!* "Yeah, okay. Answer it."

"Put it on loudspeaker," I hissed just as Axel answered.

"Hey, Pat. Hang on, just putting you on speaker." Axel put the phone down between us and hit the button. "How you doin', man?"

My dad's voice burst into the room. "Good, bud. Good. Merry Christmas."

I clapped my hands over my mouth to stop the scream that rose. I knew they were best friends, but to hear my dad actually talking on the other end of Axel's phone was the weirdest, most surreal thing ever.

Axel shook his head at me and put his finger to his lips to shush me.

I nodded but kept my hands clamped over my mouth.

"Merry Christmas to you, too. How was your day with the family?" Axel asked.

"Oh, it was great, actually. Too much food. Gonna need to train twice as hard this week."

"Is that why you're calling?" Axel asked with grin. "Trying to work off the Christmas cookies?"

"Well, not just the cookies, but yeah. If you're free we can meet at the health club, or I can come to your place if you want to go for a run again."

Panic set it and I slid off the couch and stood up. My heart was pounding, and I couldn't stop shivering. *This was so bad!*

Axel lay back against the couch and fisted his hands on his thighs. But when he answered, his voice was relaxed. His posture definitely wasn't. "Oh, I'd love to buddy, but I've actually got someone here. That woman I told you about."

"The one you're totally into?" Dad asked with a laugh.

"Shut up," Axel growled, his gaze flicking up to me. "I'm not that bad. Can we catch up later, or maybe this weekend?"

"Sure," Dad said. "You go enjoy her. At least one of us is getting some."

"Thanks, Pat." Axel said, his gaze lifting up to meet mine. "See you later."

He hung up, and I screamed, the tension inside my heart too intense to contain. "Oh my God!"

Axel jumped to his feet and grabbed my arms. "It's okay. Calm down."

I twisted out of his grasp and started pacing around the room, throwing my hands up in the air like I was the main act in a pantomime. "What the hell are we going to do?"

Axel was too calm when he asked, "What do you mean?"

"What do you mean, what do I mean? My dad almost caught us together! Imagine if he'd just come over. I would have been here, and he would have—"

"Chastity, relax."

I growled and rolled my eyes but didn't respond. *Relax?* How was I supposed to relax?

"He didn't come over and catch us," Axel said, calm as a cucumber. "We're not doing anything wrong. You don't need to feel so worried. Or guilty."

I stopped pacing and turned around and glared at him. "Not doing anything wrong? Are you kidding me?"

"We're not," Axel said, his gaze burning into mine with an intensity I didn't totally understand. "We're two consenting adults. We're dating. It's no one else's business what we do in our free time."

I put my hands on my hips. "Then what was that stuff about the girl you're seeing? Are you dating someone I don't know about, or did you actually tell my dad about me?" There was no way they'd been talking about me, and I hated the fact my father knew what sort of guy Axel was. One who rolled from one woman to another the same way I went from one good book to the next.

"I'm not seeing anyone else," Axel growled, his hands tightening into fists.

Oh, he was angry, was he? What the hell did he have to be angry about? I inhaled and poured all my frustrations about this situation into words. "Well, how would I know?" I threw back at him. "We aren't exclusive. There haven't been any promises made. In fact, I think the only thing you *have* promised me is that these two weeks will be nothing to you. That you'll walk away and not look back."

Axel stalked towards me, and I found myself backing up until my spine hit the wall behind me.

I gasped as he didn't stop his approach.

Instead, he pressed his body into mine, hard, against the wall. Then put a hand on either side of my head as he stared down at me. "You want promises, Chastity? Fine! I promise that you'll never forget these two weeks or me. I promise that after tonight you'll wake up with bruises all over your body from my teeth. I promise you... that there is no one else for me. Only you."

I gasped at the imagery Axel's words evoked, heat pouring through me and desire whipping my already sensitized nerves into a frenzy. I opened my mouth to say something back, but I didn't get a chance to respond.

HE SLAMMED his mouth down on mine and thrust his tongue into my mouth in the most possessive move I'd ever felt from him, effectively silencing me. But I had *a lot* to say, and so many more effective ways of telling him how I felt.

So, I grabbed his shirt and lifted it up, wanting to feel him. I ran my hands over his hard abs and flat chest, luxuriating in the heat and size of him.

Axel groaned against my mouth, then brought his arms down to cup my face and kiss me harder.

I wanted him, and I wanted him now. I grabbed his jeans, popping the one button with a flick of my wrist, and unzipping him carefully.

He wasn't wearing any boxers or briefs, so instead of encountering another layer to push through, Axel's cock sprang out and bounced against me.

I moaned at the feeling, unable to help it. I loved the feel of his hot, hard shaft in my hand.

Axel pulled back from our kiss and stared down at me, a question clear in his eyes. *Did I really want this?*

In answer, I tugged on his cock, reveling in the gasp and groan he gave me. I'd worn a short skirt and T-shirt and as Axel reached under my skirt to slide his hand into my panties, I wished I'd worn something even more accessible.

He slid his fingers over my clit, making me gasp and fall against him with need. Then he kissed me again and thrust his fingers in and out of me in the same way that I ached for his cock.

"Oh, please," I gasped against his lips.

He pushed me up against the wall and lifted me.

I jumped up higher and wrapped my legs around his waist.

He pushed my underwear aside and set his cock at my entrance.

I shivered, needing him so much.

Then he looked at me and connected our gazes in a way that meant I couldn't look away. I didn't dare.

So, I stared into his dark eyes as he thrust into me.

"Oh. My," I gasped out as he drove into me again and again. I pulled him closer, biting his lip and kissing him hard as his cock filled me up, making me ache—and soothing that ache—all in one fast primitive dance. It was hard. And fast. And hot. And when I came, I screamed and clung to him like a limpet on a rock.

Axel followed me moments later. He groaned and pulled out, holding me tight against him as he came.

Running my hands through his hair, I dug my fingers into his back, never wanting him to leave. I didn't want him to speak and didn't want him to put me down. I just wanted to stay here, enjoying the sound of our panting filling the air and the incredible sense of female satisfaction that came with knowing my man wanted me this much.

"Are you okay?" he whispered.

I nodded and forced my eyes to open. "Oh, yeah."

"Are you sure I didn't hurt you?"

I laughed as I cupped his cheek and stared at him. He was worried about me. Well, time to reassure him that I was more than fine. "Definitely another fantasy fulfilled."

Axel chuckled as he took a step back and I let my legs slide to the floor while he still held me.

My legs were unsteady and wobbled like jelly, so I leaned back against the wall, my belly still tight with after-tremors.

"And which fantasy was that?" he asked, picking up his clothes and arching an eyebrow in question.

"Ah..." I tilted my head, trying to get my messy thoughts into line. "The one about having hot sex against a wall."

He held out his hand and I took it, grateful to have contact again. "Well, how about we get clean, share a shower, then climb into bed for round two?"

"Yes, please," I managed to say, though my usual post-sex drunkenness had hit. I could barely walk, let alone string together a decent sentence.

We staggered to the bathroom and were soon in the hot shower. He washed me while I let pleasure pulse through me. Axel always made me feel incredible, and I was already dreading the day I didn't have an evening with him to look forward to.

"Let's get you into bed before you fall over."

I nodded in agreement, my eyes at half-mast. I was having real trouble staying awake after that orgasm.

Axel dried me with his big, fluffy towel then patted me on the ass. "Go on. Get under the covers and I'll be there in a minute."

I nodded and staggered towards the door, then the massive bed. The sheets were clean but smelled of Axel too. He definitely hadn't had a woman in this bed since I'd left. Or he'd changed the sheets for me. Either way, I didn't have the energy to care at this point in time. I rolled onto my side and cuddled into the warm blankets, listening to the sounds Axel made from the bathroom as he dried himself, whistling happily as he turned off the lights and slid in behind me.

"Do you want a cat nap before the next round?" Axel whispered into my ear as he dropped a kiss on my hair.

My eyes were already closed. "Yes, please."

Axel settled into the bed behind me and slipped his arm around my waist, holding my breast in a classic male show of possession.

I smiled to myself, loving it probably more than I should.

"Can I ask you... why was me taking you against a wall part of your fantasy list?"

I sighed. It was difficult to explain, but I may as well try. "It wasn't the position so much as the passion. I wanted you to take me without any thought or preparation. It made me feel needed." I relaxed on my pillow and began to spiral down into the darkness of sleep, but I could have sworn that I heard him say something right before I passed out.

Something that sounded very much like, "Oh, you're needed, beautiful. More than you know."

33

AXEL

Chastity and I spent the rest of the day in bed, talking, eating, and having sex. I'd never had such a lazy day. When she left to have dinner with her mother, much to my dismay, I had a dozen missed calls and emails for days. But amazingly, I didn't care. Life was made for the sort of happiness I was feeling at the moment as I floated from one room to the next.

When my phone rang, I didn't even look at who it was, I just picked it up. "Hello."

"Axel, Merry Christmas."

My heart sank, which was not the reaction I should have to my parents calling to wish me happy holidays.

"Hello, Mom. Merry Christmas to you."

"Did you have a good day yesterday? I apologize for being late to call, but with the time difference, it makes it very difficult."

Oh, yes. Christmas morning was thirty-six hours ago, and the time difference of five hours to London made it impossible. "No problem," I told her, because really, why would I have expected any different? "How was your day?" I trudged to the kitchen to put on the coffee maker. I needed a pick-me-up now.

"Oh, lovely. We went to the club and had lunch, then drinks with friends. Dinner out at the hotel."

I ran my hand through my hair and closed my eyes. Trying not to snap at my mother was a constant battle. She was so superficial. So not who I wanted my wife to be. I needed someone loving, smart, and maybe a little soft. Someone I could talk to, be relaxed with. Someone like... "How's Dad?" I asked her, cutting off the inevitable conclusion my sex-drugged brain was about to make.

"He's well," she said but made no attempt to pass the phone to him, nor divulge any extra information.

"Thanks for the phone call, Mom. But I better get going. I have a call from Taiwan in an hour. Better prepare for that."

"I'm glad your business is doing well, Axel."

I inhaled sharply. It wasn't the words so much as the tone. Almost as though she was surprised that I'd succeeded without their help. In a rare moment of weakness I said, "My company turns over a billion dollars a year now, Mom."

Her tutting disapproval down the line was the reason I never told her anything. "You shouldn't talk about money like that, Axel. How... common of you."

I clenched my jaw and held my tongue. Honesty never got anywhere with my mother. "I better go, Mother. Say hello to Dad for me, and thanks for the call."

"Bye, sweetheart."

I almost gagged at the last moment, but quickly hung up. I threw the phone down on the counter and quickly made myself a coffee, weak and sweet. No point ramping myself up if I was going to bed at a normal time.

I glanced down at my phone again. Maybe Chastity would want to come back tonight? More sex? A good night's sleep. Couldn't hurt to ask, could it? I texted her a quick message and got one back within a minute.

I'd love to but I can't. Mom's already shitty at me for

not spending enough time with her. But can I come tomorrow night? Maybe stay over again?

I typed back something to say that was fine, and yeah, of course. But my chest was twisted and aching. I didn't really like Chastity's mother. I knew she was a bitch, if Pat's description of her was anything to go by. But she loved Chastity, and that was something I'd never had. A parent to adore me. Which would make Chastity a great mom, I'd expect. She liked the intimacy that came with being close to her parents.

Another tick for her.

"Shut up," I growled at myself, took my coffee and headed off to my computer. After all, what else did I have to do except work? Gym, maybe? Not this late, I'd never sleep. Another woman? My phone was *filled* with booty call numbers.

Hell, no. There was only one woman I wanted in my bed, and her scent was still imprinted on the pillow. I wasn't messing with that. And that was assuming I could even get it up for someone else, which was in question at the moment.

I sat down at my computer and got to work.

Twenty-four hours later, my elevator door opened to reveal Chastity again. I was waiting on the sofa, pretending to read the newspaper. After all, there was no reason she needed to know that I'd been waiting impatiently for her for over an hour. "Hey, beautiful!" I called out, folding the paper and placing it on my coffee table. "How was your day?" I stood up and stared at her as she walked towards me in a pair of denim shorts and a pink T-shirt. She was delicious, all luscious curves and sun-kissed skin.

"Good." She dropped her bag on the sofa, going up on her tip toes to kiss me.

I didn't let her go, instead gripping her tiny waist and pulling her close for a longer kiss.

She smiled against my mouth, then pressed in closer, opening her mouth to my tongue and moaning in pleasure as I kissed her deeper.

When I finally lifted my head, she was grinning up at me. "I love how you kiss me."

I couldn't stop the answering smile that tugged at my lips. "How do I kiss you, exactly?"

"Like you really want to kiss me."

I laughed. "Of course, I do, or I wouldn't do it."

She shrugged, running her hands up and down my arms. "Well then, all the other guys I've kissed didn't really want to kiss me."

I couldn't contain the envy that clawed at me at her words. "How many guys are we talking about?"

She stared straight at me and raised an eyebrow. "How many women have you kissed?"

Kissed? She had to be kidding me. "A gentleman doesn't kiss and tell."

"And neither does a lady." She gave me a definitive nod and I chuckled again. I loved the fact she wasn't intimidated by me. Chastity always told me what she was thinking and wasn't worried about offending me either.

"Are you hungry?" I asked, taking her hand and tugging her towards the kitchen.

"Not really." She ran her hand along the white marble countertop. "Can I ask you something?"

"Anything," I answered, though if it was another question about my past lovers, I was pretty sure I was going to avoid it like the plague.

"Why don't you have any staff? Don't rich guys have housekeepers? Cleaning ladies? Chefs?"

I pushed my hands into the cold marble and glanced around the stainless-steel kitchen. "Yeah, they do. And I have a cleaner come once a week."

She grinned at me. "But what about other staff? Don't you have a cook at least?"

I shrugged. "I don't really need one. I live here alone. I'm pretty neat and self-sufficient." To an anal level, if my ex-girlfriends were to be believed. I tilted my head at her. "Why? Do you think I should?"

She shook her head. "Not at all. I was just wondering, that's all."

I went to the fridge. "Want a beer? Or a wine, or something?"

I kept everything pretty stocked. Or my assistant at work did. I had several, and I suppose in a way, they doubled as personal staff. They ordered groceries and organized restaurant reservations.

"No, thank you."

I turned to stare at her. "Anything you'd like do then?"

She grinned at me. "Yeah. I want to make love to you."

I put the beer back in the fridge and picked her up. "Well, why didn't you just say so?" I carried her to bed and made love to her the way she wanted me to. Slowly. Thoroughly. As though we had all the time in the world. And tonight, we did.

34

CHASTITY

I woke up to the feeling of Axel's hard cock pressing into my butt crack and his hands tweaking my nipples. I giggled and bumped my ass back into him. "You want some more?"

"Hmmm... always."

I was so warm, but I was also really wanting to complete my bucket list. "Could we have sex on the kitchen counter?"

He stopped tweaking my nipples and froze. "Uh... what?"

I twisted onto my back and stared up at him. "You know I have my fantasy list, and I want to get through everything before I go back to school."

Axel groaned. "Don't talk like that."

"Like what?"

"Like you're leaving tomorrow."

I bit my lip and stared up at him. He didn't want me to go, that was damn certain. But would he consider continuing this relationship once I returned to school? Two hours was a decent drive, but not insurmountable. And long-distance had a bad reputation for never working, but if he was extremely busy with work and was okay with me coming back for weekends, surely we could try?

He sighed. "I'm sorry. You're right. Let's do it."

He slid out of bed, and I sat up. "I killed the mood, didn't I?"

"No... It's not your fault. I'm just... not looking forward to you leaving."

I threw back the covers and got to my feet. "Neither am I."

He smiled wickedly and held out his hand. "Well, let's go make some memories."

I hurried over to him and took his hand. Making memories with him was the only thing that was keeping me from bursting into tears at the prospect of not seeing him again.

We walked over to the kitchen and Axel grabbed a hand towel and popped it onto the counter. "Can't let that gorgeous ass get cold."

He grabbed me around the waist and hoisted me onto the counter. "Oh! It *is* cold."

He grinned as he pushed my knees apart and stepped between them. "You won't be cold for long."

Happiness surged through me as he leaned closer to kiss me.

His lips touched mine and I sighed, running my hands over his shoulders, loving the sturdy muscles beneath my palms.

Vaguely, I heard a sound, then footsteps penetrated the bubble around me.

"*Chastity?* What the hell are you doing here?"

I gasped and pulled back, covering my bare breasts with my arms. "Dad!"

Axel twisted his body to cover mine, putting his back to my father. "Pat, go wait in the living room."

"Axel. What the fuck?"

"Just go. We'll be there in a minute."

Dad stomped away and I stared up at Axel's face, panic-stricken. My stomach was lurching, ready to vomit. And my heart was pounding with a sickening thud. "Oh my God. What are we going to do?"

Axel stepped away, and all signs of the passionate man I'd known only moments before were gone. "We're going to face the music," he answered. "Though, I think we better get dressed first."

35

CHASTITY

I was shaking. Literally shaking like a leaf in the wind.

Like a girl whose father just caught her having sex with his best friend. Thank God we'd only just started! It could have been so much worse.

"It's okay," Axel said, pulling on a sweatshirt and some pants.

"It's not going to be okay," I managed to say, though my throat ached, and my chest hurt. "It's not. He's never going to forgive me."

Axel growled, in frustration I assumed. "We've just gotta tell him the truth. That we met way before we knew how we were connected. And by then, it was too late."

"Yeah, I suppose."

I clipped up my bra and pulled on a sweater to cover myself. I felt naked and alone. My father had seen me naked! And having sex with Axel. Surely that was too much for any father to handle. I tidied myself up the best I could, and Axel waited for me. "Thanks for covering me when he walked in," I said, crossing my arms over my chest.

"What do you mean?"

I frowned at him. Hadn't he even noticed that he'd instinctively

180

protected me? "You turned your back and blocked my father's view of me. Didn't you do it on purpose?" I was sure he had.

"Uh, yeah. I suppose." Axel said, lifting his chin a notch.

Why was he acting defensively? I ran my hands through my hair and sighed. "Shall we go?"

He nodded, and together but separately we walked out of the bedroom, around the kitchen and into the living room where my dad sat in the armchair facing us. His cheeks were slashed with angry red, and when I looked at him, he glanced away as though he couldn't even bring himself to look at me.

I sank onto the sofa to the left, and Axel stood over near the sofa on the right. We hadn't worked out a strategy of what we were going to tell him other than the truth, so I had no idea how this was actually going to go. I put my hand to my mouth. I was going to be sick.

"So," my dad said, running his hands up and down his thighs in an agitated move I'd only seen on him once before. "How long has this been going on? Since my birthday?"

"No!" I said, immediately jumping in. "We met at the gym, and we had no idea who each other was. We went on a few dates and then found out that you two knew each other."

Dad sat up straighter and slid to the edge of the recliner chair. "And when you found out Axel was my best friend, what did you do, Chastity?"

I felt as small as a child sitting at the feet of a giant.

"We, ah..." I swallowed hard. "We broke up."

Dad jumped to his feet, throwing his arms out wide. "Then what the fuck is going on here?"

I sobbed and caught the sound by covering my mouth with my hand again. *Dad, I'm so sorry.* My stomach was clenched so tightly now, it felt twisted.

Axel gripped the back of the chair, and my traitorous gaze swept over his magnificence.

Even as terrified as I was for my relationship with my dad, I still couldn't stop myself from admiring how good Axel looked standing there, tall and handsome.

"Pat, look. I'm sorry you had to find out this way. Not ideal in any way."

"Not ideal?" Dad repeated, his gaze narrowing on Axel. "You were up here *fucking* my daughter, Axel."

Axel put his hands up in surrender. "I'm sorry, Pat."

"You're not sorry." Dad groaned, then put up his hand to stop Axel from speaking. "And you have no idea how I feel, Axel. No idea!"

"No, I don't," Axel said, his tone calm.

I curled up tighter on the couch, bringing my knees up and wrapping my arms around my legs.

"No, you don't. Because you don't have any kids," My dad hissed. "And why don't you?"

"I'm sure you're going to tell me," Axel muttered, glancing down at the carpet at his feet.

"Because you're a selfish, narcissistic asshole."

Oh, no, you don't! "Dad!" I unfurled and jumped to my feet. "You can't talk to him like that."

My dad whirled on me. "I've known Axel since you were in elementary school, sweetheart. You don't get to tell me how I speak to him."

Tears blurred my vision, and I fought back the cry that lodged in my throat. "But, Dad—"

"No!" My father growled at me. "I'm disgusted with you. Disgusted with you both."

Then he turned his gaze on Axel. "You're twenty years older than her, for fuck's sake."

"We know that," I managed to say, coughing to clear my throat. "This was only meant to be a holiday fling. Nothing serious."

Dad pushed Axel in the chest. "You bastard. You take my daughter... MY DAUGHTER, and convince her to have some slutty affair? She's better than that, Axel, and you know it!"

"It wasn't his fault, Dad," I said, my face bursting into a hot flush. I had to tell him the truth. He couldn't blame all this on Axel. "I was the one who begged him to date me for the couple of weeks I was here. He didn't want to go on after we found out the connection, but I—"

Dad grunted at me and dismissed me with a flick of a hand. "You're a child, Chastity. You don't know anything about this guy."

My tears dried up and my mouth dropped open. I was a child? "Excuse me?"

Dad glared at Axel, who was standing placidly despite being pushed back a few feet. "You and I are done, you got it? Come on, Chastity. We're going home."

I tried not to see the hurt on Axel's face, but it was impossible to ignore. I tried again. "Dad, please stop. I know this is a shock, but I'm almost twenty-two. And I like Axel. He's been great for me."

My father finally turned towards me and gave me his full attention. "You have no idea how I'm feeling, Chastity. Shock doesn't even come close to covering it. And as for Axel, I fail to see how some rich player who's slept with half the women in the city can be good for you. You've got your whole life ahead of you."

"Dad, stop!" I gasped. "You have no idea about our relationship, or how amazing Axel has been to me."

"Yeah," My father said, rolling his eyes with an exaggerated groan. "I'm sure he turned on the charm to get in your pants, Chastity. But don't expect him to stick around. He created the saying, *'hit it and quit it'*."

Anger boiled inside of me. I knew that Axel was experienced, he had to be. He was twenty years older than me, gorgeous, single, and rich. It would be sad if it didn't have a little black book stashed somewhere.

"Stop!" I yelled, not willing to take the character assassination any longer. Axel wasn't saying a thing, but I couldn't stay quiet. "I love him, Dad. I love him! He's amazing. And even if this fling lasts only two weeks, I'm happy. How can you not see that?" Where the words came from, I had no idea.

And when both men stopped and turned to stare at me, I realized I may have overstepped the mark.

"What?" I asked, flicking my hair back over my shoulder.

"Did you just say you love him?" my father asked, his eyes wide with shock.

"Uh…" I swallowed hard. *Shit.* had I said that? "Yeah… I…"

Dad swung around to glare at Axel. "Now she loves you? Fucking hell, man! Why'd you have to go and screw with my daughter, of all people!"

Axel turned to stare at me, his mouth hard and pressed into a thin line. "That wasn't the deal, Chastity."

It was my turn to be shocked speechless.

Dad shoved Axel again. "What did you just say? She says she loves you and you say that wasn't the deal?"

Axel's eyes blazed with anger. "It wasn't! I told her what was on offer, and she was happy with it."

Dad's hand tightened into a fist, and he swung his arm in a lightning-fast move. *Cr-aaack.* Dad's fist connected with Axel's face and sent him spiraling into the sofa. "You're a smug bastard," Dad grunted, then grabbed my arm. "Let's go."

"Axel…" I didn't want to go.

Axel wiped at the blood dripping from his lip. "Go."

"But—"

His gaze flashed up at me. "Chastity. *Go.* There's nothing more to say."

I disagreed. I had so much more to tell him, share with him.

But from the hard set of Dad's jaw and Axel's equally stubborn set, I had no choice in the matter.

"Let me grab my bag," I told my father, pulling my arm out of his grip.

"Where is it?" he asked.

"The bedroom."

Dad huffed out half a laugh. "How was it sleeping in that bed by yourself all night? Bit lonely?"

I frowned at my father. "What do you mean?"

Dad crossed his arms over his chest, a malicious smile on his lips. "Everyone knows Axel won't sleep with his women. He spends more time in the guest room than his own bedroom."

I inhaled sharply, wishing I could pull my dad to the room and show him the indentation of Axel's head.

"Well, that shows just how much you don't know him, Dad. Axel's slept with me, all night, *every* night we've been together."

My father's face changed into a twisted amount of disgust and shock.

But I didn't wait for his response, I stormed to the bedroom, grabbed my bag, and marched back. "You ready?"

My dad nodded, but his demeanor had changed, and I wasn't sure what I'd said, or Axel had said to change it. It didn't matter. Axel wanted me gone, so I was going.

"We going?" I repeated as I threw my bag over my shoulder and glared at my father.

"Uh, yeah."

The wind had definitely been taken out of his sails, but I was anxious to go now.

Axel was staring towards the fireplace, his back to me.

I didn't say goodbye, instead walking straight to the elevator and pushing the button.

Dad stepped up beside me a minute later, and together we went down the lift, out the door and into his car.

I don't know how I managed to keep it all together until I was safely inside my bedroom at my mom's place, but I did. And only then did I allow the tears to fall. And after that, they didn't stop.

Continue Axel and Chastity's journey with book 2 - '***Pregnant to my Dad's Billionaire Best*** Friend.'
Download:
https://books2read.com/u/m2YrA7!

www.ingramcontent.com/pod-product-compliance
Lightning Source LLC
Chambersburg PA
CBHW070958190726

48292CB00004B/1499